Nightmare's Curse

By: Rachel and Rebecca Pittek

Jahinie Productions

www.jahinie.com

412-216-8072

Printed in the United States of America.

ISBN: 978-061-577-5722

Published by:

Jahinie Productions

www.jahinie.com

412-216-8072

This book is dedicated to all my friends and family who have supported me all the way, and made my dreams come true. Thank you so much MaryBeth, James, Rebecca, and Abby C. For this wouldn't be possible without you all.

Thank you.

Contents

PROLOGUE

The winds howl and trees bend as the storm rages across the land. Tornadoes grow from the dark clouds and lightning flashes across the sky. A shadowy figure is seen amid the chaos and destruction. The Wizard of Dark laughs as his powers grow in strength. The earth rumbles and shakes, animals become silent, and the sun's light is slowly consumed by darkness. Below the Wizard, in the clearing of the forest, is a group of women. All of them are dressed in white robes and they vary in age. One of the White Witches steps forth and cries, "Wizard of Dark, why have you done this to our land? Why are you so displeased?"

A deep, malicious laughter drowns out her cry.

"*OUR* land? How foolish you are! This land is mine and so is its power. With it I will control this planet and many others. I shall become the ultimate, THE SUPREME RULER OF ALL!" The White Witches watch in fear as their land is torn apart, all life being vanquished. They gather in a circle below the unruly tyrant and begin to bang their staffs upon the ground. One of the witches draws a circle behind the others with a white powder. In front of each of the seven witches a symbol lays before them. When the circle is complete, the circle and symbols start to glow. The staff bangs become faster and faster. A chant rises above the wind and thunder. The Wizard of Dark gazes down. All goes silent as if time came to a standstill. The wind and the breaking of trees are no longer heard. Then from the circle below, a bright, white light is released, and everything is consumed.

Chapter 1

It is All Hallows Eve but many now know of it as Halloween. The night where children come out dressed as something they are not. Some are glittery with white wings while others are dark, bloodied, or seem to be torn to shreds. Giggles and laughter fill the night as the children ring doorbells and their candy bags start to overflow. They run from door to door repeating the same simple phrase over and over again.

"Trick or Treat!" says a group of three children. An Elderly man opens the door and greets the children with a bowl full of candy. They each reach in and grab a piece, thank the man and leave. Jack, an albino wolf, is dressed like a zombie biker with holes in his leather jacket, shredded jeans, and his wolf-like ears painted in blood. He has his fur tinted a greenish white and his shirt slightly torn. Katz, the girl next to him, is dressed as a pop star. Her bright red boa drapes around her shoulders on top of her black tube top. On top her head and behind her green cat-like ears is a feathery headband and she has a red bow tied to her tail. Scott digs through his bag looking for his favorite candy to save for later. He is dressed like a typical vampire. Scott's face is white with blood coming out the right corner of his mouth. He points his round raccoon-like ears back giving him that mysterious allure. His long dark cape flowing in the wind, just above his tail, and is fastened by a fake sapphire gem. They giggle and laugh as they talk amongst each other. A house appears in the distance with only a single jack-o-lantern sitting on a stool. It's gazing eyes and crooked smile catches Katz's eye.

"There's my grandmother's house! We can stop there for the night."

"Why? There are so many more houses to get candy from and..."

"Scott, our bags are about to explode from how much candy we got. It won't hurt if we stop."

"Katz's right. This bag is starting to hurt my shoulder. Plus there's enough candy here to keep me out of school for weeks!"

The children laugh at Jack's silly idea. He always tries to find a way to get out of school. Katz opens the door and sees her grandmother rush in from the kitchen. She notices it is just Katz and her friends. Her caring face looks like any typical grandmother but her physique is like a 20 year old. She can still run like a marathon runner and has kept herself healthy through her years.

"My, I thought you were some young whipper snappers trying to find the candy bowl." She laughs softly. Katz comes up and gives her a hug.

"No, it's just us coming in from a long night of trick or treating." Scott plops onto the floor in front on the couch and dumps his candy all over the place. "Yeah, there is enough to last us for the year!" Scott starts sorting through his candy eating every third one or so.

"Yeah, just enough to last you till the end of the week!" Jack just smiles and laughs when Scott glares at him. Then he just resumes sorting his candy. Jack and Katz both found spaces on the floor and start sorting their candy, too. They would trade stuff they didn't for something they did, and have thumb wars if two kids wanted the same candy. They chatter and laugh and Katz's grandmother calls from the kitchen.

"Dinner's done if anyone wants some real food to eat." Katz, Scott, and Jack all got up and ran into the kitchen and sat at the table. The food smells delicious.

A seasoned roast was cooked slowly in a crock pot with some potatoes and vegetables. Katz's grandmother used some of the broth cooked from the roast and made savory gravy from it to pour all over the meat and vegetables. On the side she made some salt sticks with caraway seeds. They are kind of like bread sticks but chewy like a bagel and they are great for dipping in the gravy. So they all sat down together and ate, their tummies growing warm from the dinner settling in them. After all the dinner was done and put away, Scott takes some of the leftover salt sticks and starts sopping up the gravy from the bottom of the pot.

"Well, I don't have to worry about cleaning that pot tonight. You'll have it sparkling clean before I get to it." Scott looks up from the pot with gravy all over his face and smiles goofily. The rest just laugh as Scott goes back into the pot for more.

"It's the best part! My mom lets me do this every time we have stew or anything with gravy. IT'S JUST SO GOOD!" Scott licks his lips as he finishes the last of the gravy. He fills the pot with soap and hot water and lets it sit in the sink to soak.

The candy is all sorted and back into their bags and the children sit on the couch resting after a good evening meal. Katz's grandmother came in and saw them all sitting there on the couch with smiles on their faces, especially Scott.

"You three youngsters should go for a good stroll. It is not good just sitting lettin' the fat grow on your bones."

So the three of them went out the door and wave goodbye to Katz's grandmother, but little did they know that this would be Katz's last good-bye.

Chapter 2

All the kids around town are all cozy in their homes, munching down on their candy. The lights in the houses along the streets are going out as families settle in bed for the night and the street lights light up as the sun goes down. Across from the house is a forest where Katz, Jack and Scott are walking down a dimly lit street with their flashlights, talking about the day's events. Then Jack came up with a crazy idea.

"Hey, do you guys know of the story about the castle on Old Hallows Street?' Scott shrugs his shoulders and Katz looks down at the ground with worry. Jack sighs and starts walking backwards in front of Katz and Scott.

"The story goes that on Halloween Night, a couple decided to take a walk down Old Hallows Street. This is the only street into the dark and scary forest of The Dark Pines. They walked down the dirt path until they saw something in the distance. It was a castle, The Castle of Night, standing in the middle of an empty field. It seemed nothing scurried through those fields at night. The couple walks up to the castle, looking worn and beaten. The big gate door was scarred by some unknown attack. The couple walks inside holding each other closer. Then the noises start. Bangs and crashes were heard throughout the castle. An evil laughter echoes through the hallways. Then it all stops. A low moaning groan comes from behind them. The gate door began to close, and before the couple could get out, the door slams shut. The castle disappears into the foggy mist and the couple was never seen again."

Katz looks at Jack, frightened by the story.

"That's a bunch of bologna! That's just a myth, a legend! It was made up by the cops so no kids would go there and vandalize the place." Katz looks towards the woods with worry and doubt filling her heart.

"Then if you think it is just a load of bologna, let's go. Let's go to the castle, unless you're afraid. . . " Jack sneers at Scott as he laughs in his throat. Scott stutters a bit and looks Jack in the eyes.

"Let's go to the castle. Come on Katz let's go show him he is wrong." Katz looks at Scott then at Jack. She doesn't want her friends to think she was afraid; the teasing would go on for weeks. So she takes a deep breath and sighs.

"Okay. I'll go." Jack smiles at her answer and jumps into the air.

"All right then, let's head to the castle, shall we?" He gestures to the dirt path leading into the woods. Katz didn't realize that she was standing at the dirt road leading into the terrible woods. Jack and Scott walk in front of her and she enters slowly, looking back at the houses. Will she ever see those houses again? Would she ever see her grandmother again?

The further they walk the denser the trees are. The lights from the town were soon far away and the only lights were their flashlights and the lonely moon hanging in the black, starless sky. Tree branches pull and tug at their clothes. Katz gets entangled in a bunch of branches and it felt like hands and fingers were grabbing her and trying to take her away. Then a hand pulls her forward out of the small nightmare. Her bright, red boa left in the branches to disappear into the darkness. Then Jack let out a yelp. Scott and Katz rush up to meet him. On the ground is the street sign that reads "Old Hallows Street" in old, weather-worn letters. Straight ahead lay the old castle itself, it stands there lifelessly. A murky moat surrounds the castle and the once beautiful stained glass windows now broken revealing only more darkness. Katz looks in awe at the castle and then something catches her eye. In the window of the tall, right tower, a figure stood. Though you couldn't see its face, you felt the eyes stare right at you. Katz quickly turns away and when she looks back the figure has vanished.

"I think I saw something in that tower window. Something dark..." Jack looks at her as if she was crazy.

"Are you saying you saw *him*?"

"Katz?" Scott said with concern. Katz shakes her head and just tells herself that she just seeing things.

"...Sorry...my mind was playing tricks on me."

"Good, I thought you were losing it already. We didn't even get to the castle yet."

They walk up to the castle's great door and realize that the door is actually an old draw bridge that leads to the castle. The bridge's chains and metal show years of rust and damage. Old burn marks decorate the door as if from a war fought years ago. Bolts are missing, and there are holes in the wood that is slowly becoming dust. The kids walk carefully across the bridge. As they take each step it sounds as if the bridge would break at once. As they continue to cross, Katz gasps as she sees a shadow cross their path through the enormous door way. They all pause. Years of decay and erosion are easily seen at the door's arch way. Bricks are missing and the mortar dust floats in the moonlight. The kids flash their lights into the black opening. As they enter a loud thud is heard. They all point their flashlights to the direction of the noise revealing that a gigantic piece of brick and mortar has fallen from the ceiling.

"We need to be more careful" Jack and Katz both nod their heads.

As the darkness is lit up by their flashlights, they come to a staircase that covered in a carpet that is a dull red and frayed at the edges. The banisters and railings had beautiful, detailed carvings all the way up to the top. All of the steps look worn and well used. As Katz, Jack, and Scott walk up the stairs, creaking comes with each step. Suddenly a loud scream accompanied by the cracking of wood is heard, the boys look back to see that Katz has fallen through a weak step. They pull her back up and continue up the stairs. As they reach the top, they notice the hallway is enormous in height. To the right is a window whose stained glass is broken and faded in color. The window seal scratched up as if someone was hanging on for dear life. To the left, the hallway seemed to stretch on forever with an endless amount of doors lining both sides. They decided to enter the third door on the left, and as they opened the door bats flew up above the kids' heads. Once they recovered, they start to enter the room but realize the floor is gone! Below the broken boards seems to be an old ballroom. The floor is a pinkish brown with gray detail, but it is cracked and damaged and no longer had that beautiful sheen it once had. The wallpaper is falling off exposing decaying wood, the molding on the walls is falling off, and in every corner a cobweb takes refuge. Katz backs up into the hallway and once more sees that dark figure. This time it did not go away. She could feel its cold stare and shivers at the thought that it could be *him*. It continues to stare until it turns around and disappears through the door behind it. Katz taps the boys on the shoulder.

"Let's go look at that door way down there."

Jack and Scott look at Katz, shrug their shoulders, and agree. Katz is terrified at what she had just said. So, they continue down the hallway to the dreadful door. As they inch closer, bangs and clanks are heard. They thought it is just the old castle settling, but the noises got louder, the sounds came more frequently. Bangs and clanks became crashes and booms. They huddle closer together as they get closer and closer to the door. Then everything goes silent as they stand right in front of the door. Staring at the old, moldy door before them, Jack reaches out with a quivering hand and locks his fingers around the cold, rusted doorknob. Gently, the door glides open to the next room, revealing nothing but pitch blackness. A chilling breeze slithers out of the room and down their spines. The castle begins to rumble viciously and a deep, menacing voice yells *GET OUT!!!!!*

Jack, Katz, and Scott race down the stairs as the castle quakes. A gust of wind forces them through the door and onto the drawbridge. Jack and Scott rush to their feet and reach the edge of the bridge. The squealing chains scream out bringing the bridge to life. The next thing they knew they are staring into the black sky. The boys were knocked off balance and fell into the moat. They reach the bank and realize Katz is not with them. Scott looks up to the drawbridge and sees a hand waving in the air.

"KAAAAAAAAAAAAAAAAAATZZZ!!!!!"

Jack jumps for the edge of the bridge and takes hold of Katz's hand.

"Hang on Katz! Don't let go!!!!!"

"JACK!!! DON'T LEAVE ME!!! DON'T LET GO!!!!"

As Katz screams, the drawbridge juts up and causes Jack to lose his grip on Katz's hand.

"JAAAAAAAAAAAAAAAAAAACK!!!!"

Scott helps Jack get out of the moat. Then the boys heard a low mournful groan come from the castle. The gate is completely shut and not another sound is heard from the castle. The boys stare in shock as this dark looming mass known as the Castle of Night, shudders, its towers and walls crumbling to the ground slowly piece by piece. As Jack and Scott stand there a chill ran up their spines, a chill of true evil, of true darkness. Then the wind begins to whisper and a low rumbling sound rings throughout the field. A chant, spoken in ancient tongues, rises into the air. As the boys stare on they notice their breath coming out as smoky clouds. Jack looks at Scott who eyes continue to widen with fear. The whispering stops. A dark, black glow comes from the castle. STOMP... STOMP... STOMP... STOMP..... These stomps sound if like a thousand wooden canes hitting the hard stone of the ground. The sounds increase as the castle slowly disappears. The castle and the moat are now completely gone as if it were never there. The boys shake in the deathly silence that lingers about them. They turned and ran out of the forest.

"This never happened and we will not tell anyone."

Scott looks with disbelief.

"But what about Katz's grandmother?"

"We'll just have to say we saw her go into the forest and not come back out."

Scott nods quickly knowing a cold guilt inside has started to grow. He knows what has happened. He knows he is going to lie but what he didn't know is how he is going to live with this, cold gnawing inside of him, knowing what has happened to Katz.

The boys continue on their way home when a lady across the street calls to them. It is Katz's grandmother. She is such a nice woman to Jack and Scott, always kind, but tonight they are going to be on her bad side.

"Hi boys, where's Katz?"

The boys walk up to her with their heads hanging low. Something is wrong.

"Where's Katz? Where is Katz!?"

Jack twiddles with his thumbs as Scott stares at his feet. An awkward silence falls between them. Jack clears his throat.

"We...lost her...in the woods..."

Katz's grandmother's eyes grow with fear as if she heard Katz had died.

"What woods? WHAT WOODS!?"

"She went into the Dark Pines, the woods…Ma'am."

She drops the broom she had in her hands and stares off into the distance with her mouth gaping open. She covers her mouth, tears well up into her eyes as she stares at those dreadful woods. The warm tears fall down her soft cheeks as she looks at the boys. She couldn't believe it. As the boys depart, she went inside to her once cozy home. She sits on the couch by a table with a lit candle upon it. *He finally got my little Katz…my lovable Katz,* she thought. Now only the moon lit up the home that is now shadowed in darkness.

Through the deep and shadowed forest of the Dark Pines, over broken branches and scattered stones, across a river that has gone dry of water and life to an open field, a field that once was the home to the Castle of Night, now stands a figure. It is nothing more than floating darkness with red glaring eyes. It stands there in the open field with the moon drifting away. The fields becoming darker and darker until only those cold, red staring eyes continue to linger watching the entrance to the forest, to its home.

Chapter 3

Thoughts spinning violently in her head, voices muffled and screaming, swirls of faces, evil laughter, and then it went black, but not for long. Something in the distance is beginning to appear and yet something feels wrong. The image started to become clear and red. It is those eyes she has seen before. She turns away to have something make her turn back. Suddenly the eyes are straight in front of her, evil laughter fills the air, a force grabs her and she gasps for breath. Katz jumps up from the floor she slept upon. Her heart races and she remembers those red eyes that which are now scorched into her mind. Katz stands up to look at the room that entraps her. A single bulb hangs in the air and only lights up the center of the room. A broom sits covered in dust and cobwebs with a beaten, splintered door that looms there, never to open. Katz curls up in the corner furthest from the door. She rubs the light bluish stone of her necklace between her fingers. Tears silently fall as the darkness seems to grow. Then a loud bang came from the door and startles Katz. Light seeps from the door as it creaks open revealing an oddly shaped shadow. It plops through the doorway and a creaky chuckle came from it.

"About time sleepy beauty. We've got works to do. Come with me."

"I don't want to. Leave...mmmme...alone." Katz tries to curl up tighter into the corner. The figure gives a low grunt and plops closer to her. A low growl gurgles out of its throat.

"Mys master won't be pleased. NOW COME OR ELSE!!"

Katz quivers and closes her eyes hoping it to be just a bad dream and trying to wake herself up from this terrible nightmare. Yet, when she opens her eyes she is still in that musty, dank room. Instead of fighting it anymore she stands up and follows the plopping figure through the door into the unknown. The bright light blinded her as she came out into the foyer. Katz was back in front of the large staircase, the black, red eyed figure watching from the top.

* * *

Scott is lying on his bed staring at the bland, white ceiling. Jack is sitting at Scott's desk playing with a paddle ball toy, and not doing very well at it. Silence fills the room and the only noise was the BINK BINK BINK of the ball hitting the paddle. Scott laid with a sad expression on his face and guilt in his eyes. Jack stopped playing with the toy and sat it on the desk. An awkward feeling hung in the air for a time that seemed like forever. Jack twiddles his thumbs and Scott continues to stare into an endless abyss.

"We need to find Katz."

"I told you not to bring that up. There is nothing we can do so just shut up about it." Scott sat up in bed looking at Jack with a look of disbelief.

"We could ask Katz's grandma to help us. You know we can do something. I can't take this guilt anymore about leaving her behind and not saving her. That's it!" Scott picks up his jacket off the floor and heads for the door. Jack grabs and spins Scott around by his shoulder. They both stare at each other as silence lingers between them. With his hand still on Scott's shoulder, Jack's face ready to pound him, softens. Scott was about to turn and leave until Jack spoke.

"I'm sorry..." Scott feels a little uneasy with what Jack had said, but shakes it off and smiles.

"Let's go help find Katz." Jack nods and they both rush out the door.

It doesn't take long to get there but they hesitate as they reach the door. Jack rings the doorbell and a beautiful tune swims through their ears. Jack smiles but soon fades as the door opens. Katz's grandmother stands there and looks like she hasn't slept in days and had too much coffee, her eyes show a broken heart. She clears her throat and wipes a smudge off her cheek.

"Is there something you boys want?"

Her pleading eyes wait for an answer. Scott begins to speak but Jack butts in.

"We're here...to help you find Katz."

Then her eyes begin to water and gleam as she hears those words, she steps out and hugs the boys. Tears fall down her cheeks but this time they are joyful.

* * *

Katz cringes in fear at those red eyes. Then she looks down at that oddly shape figure that had led her out of the room. It was a hat!? It was a dusty, blackish-gray and a little tattered and torn around the edges. There was a dull purple patch on the very tip. Yet as it turned to her she steps back in shock. It had large red eyes with black diamond-shaped pupils and huge sharp pointed teeth. It turned back around to face the figure.

"Shesss was a bit difficult to bring out massster. What shalls we do with her?"

The dark figure looks at Katz and studies her for a moment and smiles. A low rumble came from the figure.

"We will put her to work but, for now show her to her new sleeping quarters."

Then the figure vanishes. Katz feels a tug on her leg. She looks down to see those big red eyes staring back at her.

"Followss mes."

The hat plops away and Katz slowly follows behind. It took her down a flight of stone stairs into a cold and murky atmosphere. Down the hallway an old wooden door with a small barred window stood marking the entrance into the room. It had no doorknob and yet the little hat opened it. It stepped out of the way and pointed with its brim into the room. Katz hesitates until a low growl rises from the hat. She cautiously enters the room. It had an old rusty boiler, a single light hanging from the ceiling, and another small barred window too high to reach and escape through. The door slams behind her and she tried to push it open but it wouldn't budge. The light fizzles out and now she was only left with the moon's soft glow. She slumps down into the only lit corner and falls wearily to sleep. Then abruptly

Katz is awoken by noises and voices below her. She softly lays her ear to the floor and listens. She hears that terrible voice and yet another.

Down in a locked room a figure is seen pacing back and forth. This man has been held captive in this room for many years. He is wearing black shoes, black dress pants and a white puffy dress shirt with two red ruby cufflinks on each sleeve. Over his shirt is a red vest that is black on the back and tucked into his vest is a black silk ascot with a red gem sitting at the crest of the vest. He has gray fur with white hair that is slicked back. The rug he was pacing on once had beautiful hues of reds and gold but now is dull and bland. It's seems like the colors have drained right out of it. A makeshift bed sits the corner of the room. Most of the furniture in the room is worn and faded from age. The fabric is torn and fraying and springs are pushing against the cushion's surface, yet there was one chair that seemed not affected by age at all. It still held its beautiful colors and was in the shape of a throne. It had a deep red color with bronze detail and gold tassels hanging from it. The chair is illuminated by an old fireplace with a waning fire. On top of its dusty mantle sat a vase that holds a flower. Not just any flower, but a Moon Rose. It is a white rose that glows with a bluish-purple hue. The petals sparkle in the dim light. The wolverine-like man looks up at the rose with his gaze full of sadness and loss. He takes the rose in his hand and twirls it in his fingers. A sweet heavenly aroma fills the air. The fragrant, lovely, and innocent looking rose holds a dark past. The man cringes, folding his ears back; he looks back at the rose as he puts it back into its vase.

"You're stills starin' at that putrid thing?" He looks down to see Hat staring right back.

"Leave me alone and get out of my room." Hat just smiles. The man just looks away with disgust.

"What? You're stills mad about what *he* did to yous? Are yous mad that he took your home and killed..."

"Don't you dare say it! Now leave!"

"Do yous miss that mistress, that weakling?" A loud roar came from the man as he grabs a log and throws it at Hat. Hat jumps out of the way but the man came up from behind him. The man grabs Hat from the top of his head and holds him away. He huffs and puffs with pure anger. He wanted to tear that hat to pieces. As he reaches out to grab Hat the door slams open. A cold, chilling breeze passes through the door and past the dark, looming figure. Its red glowing eyes pierce into him. Hat wiggles out of the man's grip. They both stare at each other in silence. The man's anger grows as the figure moves closer. The man lunges at the figure and flies right through him and slides across the floor. The figure levitates him and throws him into the couch and knocks it over. The man gets back up and tries again and again to hit the figure but either its dodges it or he goes right through him. The man eventually became exhausted and the figure grips him by the throat. The man just looks straight back.

"This is my house and I want you out!" the man chokes out but the figure just chuckles. The man tries to stay strong but a force pierces his heart and fills it with fear.

"You took everything away from me, Nightmare. Even her..." He looks over at the rose in its dusty vase.

"She was nothing to you."

"Yes she was! She..."

"She was weak and pathetic. She is worthless just like you, Vladmir. Now if you act up again be prepared for the worst."

Vladmir drops to the floor gasping for air as Nightmare turns to the door and exits. Hat follows behind him and laughs. The door slams shut and extinguishes the fire. The warmth left the room leaving only loneliness to linger. Vladmir looks about the room and sees nothing but destruction. Everything is overturned and smoke slithers out of the fireplace. Sadness overwhelms Vladmir and he stares into the darkness as loneliness enters his heart once more.

Katz sits up after the noises had ceased. Katz didn't hear much of the conversation but all she knows is that things seem to be worse than they appear. A cold chill runs down her spine and she realizes that this figure, who calls himself Nightmare, is evil and merciless.

Chapter 4

Katz has officially lost track of how many days she has been prisoner to this mysterious host, who she found out one night is named Nightmare. To keep her busy she is put to cleaning duties. She has to clean the floors, scrub the carpets, dust furniture, and so on. Hat usually keeps an eye on her to make sure she is doing her duties but half the time it is nowhere to be seen. But now she sees a figure that always seems to stand in the shadowed corners of the room. He doesn't say anything but just watches. After hearing the argument she knew that this man's name is Vladmir. Vladmir always has no expression on his face but his eyes always show unhappiness. Katz gets up and tries to talk to him but he vanishes. Throughout the week Katz keeps on trying to talk to Vladmir and he disappears every time. So one day when she sat on the floor with her cleaning supplies and stared at the corner where Vladmir usually appears.

"You should start your cleaning before *he* gets mad." Katz whips around to see Vladmir standing in the opposite corner of the room.

"Why are you watching me?"

"Because, while Hat is not around I'm supposed to watch you."

"Why are you here?" Vladmir stands there silently and watches Katz.

"Hello? Did you hear me?"

"Yes, but I don't have to answer." Katz huffs and continues to her cleaning duties as Vladmir supervises. She scrubs the floor for what felt like hours. Her arms became tired and sore from scrubbing so hard. The dirt seemed to be embedded into the paint. Katz sits back on her heels and sighs. She looks about the room. The kitchen's wooden cupboards and drawers are just falling apart. The paint is chipping off and slivers of wood are strewn across the floor. Ancient grease and grime covers the old fashioned stove. Rust has taken over the racks that hold up old pots above the flames. The knobs on the front are cracked, gone, or covered in grime. The room is dimly lit by two lights hanging from the ceiling. Katz looks to her left and sees a clock but she realizes that it doesn't work. So, she just goes back to work until her ears hear an annoying sound. It is that dreadful PLOP PLOP sound of Hat coming its way. Hat plops over in front of Katz who is sitting on her heels, arms crossed, and looking away. Hat just rolls its eyes and grunts.

"He wants yous back in your room. Its beddy-bye time." It chuckles with a sarcastic smile. Katz couldn't believe she is being treated like a child but she didn't want any trouble so she obeys. Katz is lead back down to the musty boiler room. There sat a plate with some bread and cheese and a glass of water. Katz didn't realize how hungry she was until she starts to chow down. She looks back up to see Vladmir and Hat watching her. She looks down with her cheeks growing red with embarrassment. Both Hat and Vladmir leave the room and Hat slams the door. The food in Katz's throat becomes a lump. She feels cold and alone once more. Katz begins to remember her friends and her grandmother. She takes hold of her necklace that her grandmother gave to her. It is the only thing from home she can truly touch. This depressed feeling slithers throughout her body and made her food become tasteless. She moves to the corner by the boiler to warm up but her cold sadness keeps the warmth at bay. She looks towards the center of the room where the moonlight creates the shadow of the bars that keep her captive. Katz watches as the light fades in and out as she slowly falls into her dreams of home.

As the days continue with no end, eventually everything became monotonous. Day in and day out she just cleans. Katz hasn't seen Vladmir for days but the stupid hat seems to be there more often than usual. Even though Vladmir didn't say much his presence is more comforting to be around. A small tear falls down her cheek followed by Hat's chuckle.

"Are you crying?"

Katz looks over to see the sarcastic smile on its face.

"Your sssuch a baby! Oh, Vladmir, oooooh Vladmir!"

Hat chuckles up a storm. Katz throws an angry look at Hat and he breaks out into cackling laughter. Katz felt her anger swell up inside her, so she picks up the bucket and drenches Hat. Hat stares up at Katz and hic-cups a bubble. Katz giggles at Hat's shocked expression. Hat plops away feeling soggy to its brim and grumbling to itself. Katz just watches as he leaves the room and just smiles. This reminded her of something her friends would have done.

Then she sighs looking at the farthest corner of the room. Vladmir has still not shown himself. Katz goes to the foyer to sweep up the layers of mortar dust that have been laying there for centuries. She looks up at the wooden gate that blocks her way to freedom and brings back the last memories of her friends. As she looks about the room it still looks the same but with all the cleaning it seemed to bring back a little life to the place. Katz smiles and continues to sweep. A cool, chilling, but light breeze blows and slithers around her body. She turns to see a shadow in the far corner. It's Vladmir but something wasn't right. His eyes are no longer filled with sorrow but lifeless emptiness and his smile full of hate. He continues to stare as he walks towards Katz. Katz notices the ruby that holds his cloak around his shoulders is dull and gray. It shines as a stone with no life, dark and endless like his stare. Katz gasps in horror as Vladmir comes closer, each footstep echoing throughout the castle and each time becoming louder. At last Vladmir and Katz are face to face. The silence is broken by a deep chuckle creeping out of Vladmir's throat. He looks straight into her eyes.

"What's wrong, Katz? It is me Vladmir."

A terrible feeling quivers through her heart.

"WHAT'S WRONG KATZ? Am I scaring you?"

Katz just stares back in terror.

"Why would you think that? I'm your friend Katz."

Katz steps away from him but he continues to walk towards her. She turns and runs into the other room. It is the lower ballroom with the broken ceiling. Katz frantically looks around but there is nowhere to hide. The steady, loud steps of Vladmir are coming closer. Katz spots a doorway and runs to it. She is now in the kitchen where the back door is heavily chained and locked.

"Katz where are you? I didn't know you like playing hide and seek. I'm a very good seeker."

Kats desperately looks for a place to hide. She spots a closet by the old stove. She opens it and sees there is just enough room for her to get in.

"Katz….Kaaaaatzz, come out, come out where ever you are."

Katz shivers at the evil chuckles that fill the room around her. She quietly closes the door and squeezes into the back corner of the closet and closes the door. Her heart races faster and faster as the footsteps creep closer and closer. A door clicks and creaks open. A few steps are heard than a loud SLAM! Soft, evil chuckles linger in the air.

"Katz come out, I won't do you any harm, promise."

Katz quickly covers her mouth hoping that he doesn't hear her frighten gasps. The footsteps stop right in front of the closet door. Vladmir chuckles as he slowly turns the knob. It slowly squeals open with a soft click revealing Vladmir. He is no longer a comforting sight and his face contorted into an evil crazed look, the horrible grinning smile becoming larger. His laughter frightens Katz as she pushes into the wall behind her leaving her nowhere to go. Vladmir lashes out and grabs Katz by the wrist and pulls her out of the closet. He pulls her so close that their faces are only a few inches apart, Katz turns away closing her eyes so she doesn't have to see that horrible face.

"What do you think of my puppet, Katz?"

A figure slithers out from behind Vladmir. It is **him.** With those hatred filled, glowing red eyes that peered into Katz's. He is not standing but floating behind Vladmir. He is a ghostly black figure with glowing red eyes and a smile full of sharp teeth. What looked to be his hands where claw-like and a black hat that looked similar to Hat sat upon his head. He looks like a dark figure from a horrible dream. The only thing Katz could focus on was his eyes. The red eyes seem to simmer with pure evil. Katz shivers with fear at the sight of him. Nothing is good about him.

"Don't you like my puppet Katz? He is such a good listener." He leans forward towards her so close that their faces almost touched. Katz's entire body became cold and chilled like the warmth was sucked right out of her. Then both of his hands come from out behind his back. In them is a glass orb. An eerie purple-black glow surrounds it. An evil sneer appears on his face and Katz looks away.

"Don't be shy. I won't harm my bait."

Katz looks back in horror. Bait!? Bait for whom? An evil laughter came out of him, a laughter that no one ever wants to hear. Katz notices a similar glow around Vladmir's gem. It is the same as the orb. He is controlling Vladmir!

"Let him go...." Katz shakes as she speaks. Vladmir grabs both of her arms and Katz gasps and begins to cry. More laughter is heard from him as Vladmir's grip gets tighter. Katz cringes at the pain and remembers an old song her grandmother told her. It was a special tune that will protect you from any harm when sung. So, through her tears she begins to sing.

"Ata mae ta colus. Ata mae..." The expression on both Vladmir's and the figure's face turns to awe then grows in to anger.

"..ta pala. Ea ou tul, Lu quar ca." Vladmir starts to wobble back and forth and his hands go to his head. The figure becomes furious. Katz's blue crystal shard that hangs around her neck begins to glow.

"Ma cluah quah. Ma quah luma..."

"Stop your singing! GRRRRAAAGH!"

"Ma litna ma eta colus!" Katz continues to sing her spiritual tune as he becomes angrier with the song. Vladmir moans and groans as he falls to his knees. Katz sings her song louder but suddenly stopped by a force gripping at her neck. She is lifted up in front of the figure whose rage and anger is easily seen in his face. Katz is thrown to the floor and hits into the cabinets behind her. Vladmir falls over onto her lap. Katz takes hold of him as the figure floats over to her. He leans over until his face is directly in front of Katz's. Tears are still coming down her face as he grabs her throat.

"You shall never speak again!"A smile comes across his face as he holds Katz in his hand. Katz begins to feel a terrible burning sensation in her throat and mind and is dropped to the floor gasping for air. He turns around walking out the door dissipating into darkness. But before he completely disappears he looks over his shoulder and glares at Katz.

"From now on you will know me as Nightmare."
Nightmare fades into the darkness with his evil laugh
lingering forever in the air. Katz shakes Vladmir to try to
wake him up, but when she speaks nothing came out.
Katz stares into an endless abyss realizing that her voice
was taken away to truly never speak again. She bows
her head in silence with endless tears falling to the floor.
Hat comes into the room with the biggest smile on his
face. Katz went to go hold Vladmir but saw that he
vanished. Katz is once more lead down to her room with
the musty boiler. Hat slams the door behind her. Katz
collapses to her knees crying endlessly as the moonlight
disappears into darkness.

* * *

Katz's grandmother and the boys sat around the
kitchen table. Upon the table are many mystical looking
objects -- small bottles filled with unknown elixirs,
necklaces, medallions, gems, crystals, and three daggers.
Each dagger had a shining silver blade with gold handles.
In each handle, detailed carvings are seen showing a
story of the power within. Along the side of each blade
are ancient looking hieroglyphs. But the most
interesting thing about those daggers is the beautiful
gems placed in the middle of each one. One is an
elegant sapphire blue, another is a rich, deep garnet red,
and the other is a deep royal purple. Jack and Scott look

in awe at the ancient treasures. Scott went to grab one of the daggers but Katz's grandmother stops him.

"Sorry."

Jack and Scott both sit down waiting for what she is going to say. She picks up a small bottle with a cork in the spout. Inside is a glowing white liquid. She hands it to Scott and Jack to look at. Jack reaches for the cork to open it but she puts her hand over his.

"Do not open this."

"Why?"

"Because the liquid inside that bottle is highly explosive. Once you pull the cork you have one minute before it explodes."

Jack quickly passes it to Scott who in turn places it back on the table, gently. Then she picks up another bottle that holds a grayish, chunky liquid and passes it to Scott.

"This liquid will turn you invisible for about one hour. The only thing bad about this one is that it smells bad and tastes like chunky black licorice."

Scott looks at the bottle and shakes the stuff inside. Jack takes the bottle and opens it just a smidge and a horrific odor came out. It smelled of rotten eggs sprayed by a thousand skunks! He quickly caps the bottle and places it on the table. Katz's grandmother picks up another bottle that looks like there is nothing inside.

"This bottle contains an elixir that will heal about any wound."

She places the bottle down and picks up the dagger with the sapphire gem on it.

"The other trinkets you won't have to worry about, but these daggers are very precious and unique."

She passes Scott the dagger with the garnet red gem and gives the one with the purple gem to Jack.

"Each of these daggers holds a unique elemental power. The powers are activated by a special incantation. You must remember that you can use its powers only so much until it needs to rejuvenate. So, you must use it wisely. Come with me and I will teach you how to use them."

Katz's grandmother picks up a pale blue crystal from the table and leads the boys into the basement. She takes them to a bare wall in the basement and begins to draw a rough picture of a door with the crystal.

Also with the crystal she draws a symbol on the door that looks like this:

A white glow shimmers around the edges of the door-shaped drawing. The symbol glows green and the wall begins to crumble into a vortex in the center of the doorway. The vortex slows down leaving behind a wall of moving water. It quickly shifts direction ever so gracefully, and through the water a soft white light glimmers through as if looking at the water from within it, staring at the sun. Scott steps forward and touches the wall. It feels like putting your hand against a gentle flowing river feeling the water ripple under your hand but when he pulls his hand back it is still dry. Scott stares at his hand in amazement as Katz's Grandmother lets out a tiny chuckle and steps right through and disappears. Jack and Scott stare in confusion. Where did she go? Scott steps forward and reaches for the wall and is all of a sudden pulled in. Jack now stands in front of the wall in silence listening to the water gurgle away.

Jack takes a deep breath and jumps in. As he enters he falls to an empty space of blue hues and then hits a rushing waterfall. The waterfall swiftly flows left and right, up and down until he drops yet again into an empty space. As he falls the blues disappear and fade to black. Now floating in a black void a voice can be heard, but it's muffled as if he were under water. Jack looks towards the area where the voice calling from and is blinded by a flash of light. As he opens his eyes Jack sees Scott staring back down at him.

"You alright dude?"

Jack gets up with a moan and notices he is sitting in a grassy meadow with Scott and Katz's Grandmother standing beside him. As he stands up he realizes the meadow seems to stretch on to a forest that is far away. Jack looks around and notices an interesting flower. It has red and purple petals that spin like a helicopter. Then a bird flies by and it too is unique. It flies and moves like a hummingbird but has bright vibrant colors like a phoenix and its song is the most beautiful he has ever heard. Scott wanders up to a tree and notices something stirring in the leaves. It looks like a squirrel but also like a cat at the same time. It had deep scarlet fur with deeper red stripes going down its back. Its golden yellow eyes stare back in curiosity. Scott turns around and sees Katz's Grandmother.

"Where are we?"

"We are in a magical land. The land of Azmala."

Chapter 5

A gentle wind blows across the land as they walk across the meadow. As they enter through the trees they come to a high cliff. Deep down the hill side nestled amongst a group of trees is a small village. There are small huts whose colors had left them long ago. Each one is whitish gray with dull pink and purple lines wrapped around the roofs, windows, and doors. Some are decorated with shapes or symbols in a pale sky blue color. In the center is a campfire ring of stones. Inside the pit stands a wooden structure that holds a cauldron. A few figures are seen at the entrance to the village. Katz's Grandmother and the boys walk up to the entrance and as they reach the entrance, eight ladies in white robes greet them. Their robes are decorated similar to the little huts and each had a symbol upon their right cheek.

"Ulma Latka Sivanna." One of them speaks and the boys gave each other confusing looks. Katz's Grandmother just smiles.

"They are welcoming us. Fellow Elders, they do not speak our language, they speak English."

"Alright Elder Sivanna. Welcome home."

Jack looks at Sivanna who takes a cloth from her pocket and wipes her cheek. Scott and Jack realize that Katz's Grandmother belongs to this tribe.

"Elder Sivanna, a fellow Elder is sick. She wishes to see you."

The Elders lead Sivanna and the boys to a hut in the far back of the village. Sivanna enters with the boys behind her, the other Elders stand outside.

"Elder Sivanna, you're here."

A weak voice came from the bed in front of them. A fragile, pale woman lies under the sheets. She reaches her hand out and Sivanna places her hand against hers. A glow of a pale blue light glows and quickly vanishes.

"Elder Niah, what happened?"

Niah's exhausted eyes slowly look at Sivanna. A deep, long sigh escapes her lips.

"Dear Elder Sivanna, I have fallen ill to an unknown disease. It weakens me slowly. I was afraid that we would not meet for one last time."

A raspy, dry cough shakes her as she recomposes herself. A small tear falls down her right cheek.

"I'm afraid that my time is drawing to a close." Niah turns over a pillow beside her and a box is revealed. The box is beautiful. The sides are plain but the lid is decorated with wondrous designs. Flowers, vines and symbols twisted, rising from its surface. There are two roses on either side of a coin-shaped design in the middle. Smaller flowers and endless vines trace the edges of the box. Below the roses and the coin are symbols. Jack and Scott couldn't make out the symbols' meaning but Sivanna did. Niah passes the box to Sivanna and sighs. Her eyes close and a final tear falls. Sivanna bows her head and whimpers out a quiet cry. Scott puts his hand on her shoulder. Sivanna looks up to his smiling face. She stands up, takes the box, and leaves the hut.

As the night draws near a deep blue serpent shines across the sky bringing the dark of night with it. Soon the sunlight is replaced by the light of the moon. Stars fill the night sky with their glow. Their gentle light lies over the small village in the deep valley. The forest seems dark and mysterious but it is only filled with sleeping life. The Elders, Jack, and Scott sit near the fire pit in the middle of the village. The oldest of the Elders stands up, her body resting on her cane. She looks at everyone who surrounds the crackling fire. She bows her head and clears her throat. A raspy voice came from her lips.

"Dear Elders, our fellow sister, Elder Niah Lumow, has left us today. She fought long and hard against the ailment that invaded her body. It was a long struggle, but tonight let's not wallow in sorrow and unhappiness for her. Let us be happy and joyful for she will be with our past Elders who will welcome her. They will keep her safe in Akmayol. We all will see her one day. Now, let us go to her home and send her to the open hands of our goddess Luma Guah."

All the Elders, hooded in their robes, stand up and follow one by one down the moonlit path. Jack and Scott follow behind Sivanna. As they marched to Elder Niah's home the Elders whisper and hum an ancient tune. One of the Elders is swinging a lantern with smoke slithering out from its openings. The rest carry glowing crystals of different colors swinging them like pendulums. Before they reach the hut two of the Elders circle the hut laying down white powder. Where the north, south, east, and west would lay, different symbols are drawn within the circle. Inside the hut Elder Niah's body remains and all of her belongings. The Elders encircle the hut. Sivanna tells Jack and Scott to stand off to the side and then joins back with the Elders. They all bow their heads, hold hands, and begin to hum. The humming became louder and louder with a quieter echo. A few of the Elders start to chant. The crystals start to float and change color. Smoke starts to rise from the white powder that surrounds the house. Jack and Scott jump back as the bright roaring flames rise from the earth. The flames slither and surround the hut. The symbols and pictures on the hut slowly fizzle into nothing. The windows flow with grayish-black smoke. The Elders chant and chant and chant. Then the flames and smoke rise above the house swirling and swirling. Then it shoots towards the ground throwing dust into the air. When the dust clears the whole entire hut is gone. The white powder along the ground disappears with a gentle wind. The Elders bow their heads, fold their hands, and walk back to the fire pit. Once they reach the pit the eldest Elder orders everyone to go home and rest for tomorrow will bring another day, another life.

* * *

Katz has been through much work since that incident. She has to wash every floor, dust every knick-knack, clean the fireplace, and much, much more. Even worse, that stupid, obnoxious hat has to keep an eye on her all day. He comes to wake her up and leaves her when she returns to her room. Her days are constant tortures of silence and sorrow. She cries every night when she returns to her dreary room. Katz knows that she must be strong but each day seems to pile more and more anguish on her shoulders. It has been weeks since she has seen any sign of Vladmir. Katz wishes to see his sweet smile to brighten up her day a little. But she has noticed that Nightmare has been appearing here and there. He doesn't say anything or approach her. Nightmare just stands at a distance and watches. Today he is in the foyer with Hat at the top of the once elegant staircase. He stays there with his arms crossed leaning back towards the wall. Nightmare just stares with an expressionless face, his red eyes constantly watching her. Katz can feel those dark eyes looking through her as if Nightmare could read her thoughts. She just continues her work cleaning and polishing the floor. Katz looks back cautiously to see if he is still standing there. A chill is felt in her heart as she slowly turns, but when she looks back he is gone. There is no sign of him or Hat. Then she hears voices coming from a room near the stairs. Katz could hear Nightmare's voice talking to Hat. She got up quietly and stands close to the door to listen in on the conversation.

"What iss bothering youss master? Isss there something wrong?" Nightmare is quiet, pondering in thought as he stands near the desk.

"You seemed to be....uh...worried." Nightmare's eyes shoot open and glare at Hat. Hat's face quickly changes to terror. Nightmare sighs and closes his eyes once more. Silence lingers between the two that seems to last for hours. Hat just looks about the study from the dull brown desk he sat on. Dusty old books sat on dusty old shelves which stood on a torn and decrepit carpet. The window's light is blocked by a heavy dark curtain. The only light emitted in the room comes from a single lamp at the far corner of the desk. Hat fiddles with the brim of himself looking between himself and Nightmare, waiting for a break in the silence. Nightmare lets out an angered sigh and looks up at the ceiling. Then he looks back at Hat who is looking back very nervously.

"They know we have that girl. Hmmmm. I can see them preparing two boys with magic and that witch is helping them." His fists slam against the surface of desk. Nightmare lets out an angry growl as he pushes the books off the desk letting them fall into a dust cloud.

"That pathetic, annoying witch, they are preparing for something!" Nightmare smiles as a soft chuckle escapes him.

"No matter how much they prepare or train, those worthless specks will not win! No one can beat me! Just wait until that fateful day because it will be their last!" Nightmare laughs maniacally. Katz backs away with that laughter ringing in her ears. Who was he talking about? What two boys? A witch? Magic? Questions flutter around in Katz's mind. Then a sudden chill of realization fills her soul. Her eyes blur with tears as the thoughts came to her. Was he talking about my friends? My Grandmother?

* * *

Jack and Scott are standing out in an open field. The sky is blue with no clouds in sight. The sun shines warmly on the field waking the sleeping life within it. Small creatures scurry through the tall grasses and the phoenix-like birds color the sky with shades of the rising sun. Scott takes a deep breath of cool air. A smile gratefully shines on his face. Jack gives Scott a nudge with his arm.

"Enjoying the sunshine are we?" Jack chuckles and looks up to the sky.

"Jack……Scott…" The boys look behind them and see Sivanna. She is now dressed like all the other Elders in the village, a robe-like gown with pale blue and lavender designs and symbols. Sivanna signals the two boys to come over to her. When the boys meet up with her, they see a long, thin, beautifully carved box at her side. Jack looks at the box with child-like curiosity. Sivanna giggles and smiles. The three of them sit on the ground in a small circle with the box in front of Sivanna. Sivanna reaches for a latch on the box and turns it, and a quiet click opens the box. Inside the box lay three daggers on a purple, silken pillow. Each dagger has its own colored gem. One is blue, another red, and the last one purple. Sivanna picks up the dagger with the blue gem and holds it gently with two hands.

"Do you remember what I told you about these daggers?" Jack and Scott sat quietly looking at the dagger then to the ground.

"You said something like they were special or something." Jack says while scratching his head. Sivanna smiles.

"They each have unique and special powers. Each one is different from the other. I have talked with the head Elder to train you in the ways of Micga."

"Micga? What is that?" Scott asks with awe in his eyes.

"Micga is magic. You will learn certain spells and how to summon the power of the dagger." Sivanna lays the daggers with each handle touching each other in a triangle-like shape. They gleam like a mysterious treasure that was once lost with time. Sivanna closes her eyes, bows her head, and breathes deeply. Her crystal necklace rises from her chest and floats in front of her head. The crystal pulses with a yellow light. A quiet humming sound escapes from her body. The daggers begin to float in a circle with the daggers' sharp blades pointing to the sky. They spin and spin in a circle, faster and faster. The dagger with the sapphire gem falls in front of Sivanna. Jack and Scott watch in anticipation of which blade would fall before them. A bright light makes Jack and Scott turn away and when they look back the blades lay in front of them. Jack has the dagger with the royal purple gem while Scott has the dagger with the garnet gem. Sivanna's crystal falls back down to her chest and she raises her head. A smile comes to her face.

"The daggers have chosen their wielders. Now it's time to start the training process."

Chapter 6

Katz has lost the track of time. The only light she ever sees is the moonlight through the bars of her window in her room. She never sees the sunshine. Katz is now in the old ballroom. The floor is cracked and its sheen long gone. The pink paint is imbedded with years of dirt and grime. The wallpaper and paint are curling off the wall, and the paint is actually chipping off in some places. Borders and trim are falling off or hanging by a single nail. The mirrors that hang on the wall are tarnished and cracked. The ceiling is completely gone. Every corner of the room is filled with cobwebs and spiders. This place was once beautiful and must have held famous people. Katz wonders what it did look like in its hay days. The beauty of it must have been amazing. A sigh falls from her lips. She is not here to daydream, she is here to clean. Most of the castle is in better shape than it was, but everything needs either rebuilt or replaced. So, Katz gets down on her knees and starts to clean. She has to dust, wipe, clean, polish and much more to make the room better. She hears something skitter across the floor in the one corner. She looks up expecting a rat or something but it wasn't. When she looks up the only thing she sees is someone she hasn't seen in a long time -- Vladmir. He didn't come close to where Katz is kneeling. He just stands in the shadows of a dark corner staring with an expressionless face. Katz's heart flutters and she smiles but Vladmir looks away. Katz stands up and walks over to Vladmir, but again he turns away more and more as Katz's steps come closer. Katz comes up to see Vladmir's back. She feels Vladmir's sadness and guilt emanate from him. Katz softly places her hand on his shoulder and feels his shoulder relax. Vladmir looks over his shoulder at Katz. She sees the stress and depression in his eyes. Vladmir looks down and releases a deep sigh. He disappears in swirls of black smoke and Katz's hand falls. She stares into the corner with her eyes welling up with tears. Katz turns her head down, and walks slowly back and kneels on the floor. She closes her eyes as she feels her heart sink into the depths of sadness.

Vladmir is back in his chamber. The cool air fills the room with loneliness. He slouches into his chair in front of the fireplace. The fire crackles quietly over the red glowing cinders. Its warmth slowly creeps into the room as if being cautious. Vladmir's face falls into his hands as he heaves a heavy sigh, full of despair. His hurting eyes look up at the pale rose in its vase upon the mantel. Vladmir cringes as his thoughts come back to haunt him. He sees the terrified face of Katz. So much fear was shown in her face, so much terror. He balls his fists and presses them against his temples. He stands up, and in a rage slams his hands down hard on the coffee table behind his chair. The table splinters and shatters into pieces, the glass is broken into tiny shards. He glares at the rose in its vase. Anger swells and his face grows red. His vision narrows until all its sees is a single rose. Vladmir swipes his hands across the mantle knocking everything off. The glass vase spins towards the edge as Vladmir screams in rage. Then he is silenced by the gentle break of the vase hitting the floor. Vladmir looks down to see the pale rose lying in a puddle of water and glass. He kneels down on the floor and picks up the rose. He holds the rose to his face and lets the petals gently pass his cheek. Tears slowly fill his eyes and then everything comes to the surface. Vladmir shakes with grief and hopelessness. He slowly gets in his chair his head in his hands and the pale rose hanging loosely from his fingertips.

Katz is about done with the ballroom when she looks out the hole in the broken stained glass window. Outside, she saw greenery and colors. She moved around the hole to try to get a better look, but no luck. Then she remembered the big window at the top of the staircase. Katz looks around to see if Hat is nearby and there's no sight of him. So she sneaks out of the ballroom and goes up to the staircase quietly hoping no one heard her. Then the faint moonlight gleams through the window. It looms more than five times her height. She puts her hands to the glass and looks out. Katz's eyes fill with awe and inspiration. It is a courtyard full of beautiful flowers. The courtyard looks like a compass with four paths and a large fountain in the middle. In between each path flowers grew everywhere, every color known shined like a star in the dark courtyard. They twinkled and sparkled and swayed gently in the wind. Her heart feels lifted from the grief and darkness she has been in. She feels light on her feet and something catches her eye. The most beautiful flower she has ever seen. They look like roses but their hue is of pale blues and purples. The roses surround the fountain making it look like it is sitting on a cloud of flowers. Everything around her seemed to just disappear. Down below in the basement a figure is looking out a window, looking at the garden as well. Vladmir stands with his hands behind him as he looks upon his garden, such beauty in a horrible place. He notices someone else gazing upon his garden. It is Katz. He steps back but just enough to still see her. The smile on her face gleamed like the flowers themselves. She has not noticed Vladmir standing there. Vladmir looked back to the garden then to Katz whose back is now towards the window and she disappears. Hat appears in front of the window looking down at the flowers sticking his tongue out, smiles, and leaves. Vladmir growls at him and a thought pops up in his mind. There are herbs in the garden that he can use to help Katz get her voice back. Vladmir looks towards the window again and sees Hat is nowhere to be seen. So he sneaks out to the garden to get larengard flowers and nectar from an icicle flower and takes them back to his room.

Katz is now being taken back to her room. The sight of the garden will not leave her mind, the beautiful colors and so much life in the garden. Then something bumps her in the leg and she looks down to see Hat.

"Quitsss daydreamin' and get your rooms." Hat pushes her into the room and closes the door and locks it. Katz sighs and looks about her dreary room. Then something wonderful smelling catches her attention. She looks towards the floor to see by her food is a cup of hot tea. She sits down and takes a sip. She could feel the warmth fill her up. Then she looks down to see the note that was sitting underneath the cup. She opens it up and reads:

This will help but remain silent.

Chapter 7

"WAKE UP SLEEPY HEADS! TIME FOR TRAINING!"

Jack falls out of bed to the hard ground and moans. Scott rolls over, covers his head and sighs. Then all of a sudden the door slams open and the loud BANG BANG of a metal pan shakes the room. Jack covers his ears with his blanket and Scott sits up and screams.

"I DIDN'T DO IT, I SWEAR!" Scott realizes Jack and the figure at the door are staring at him. He starts to blush and hides behind his pillow.

"Sorry."

"Why did you wake us up so early Sivanna? It's too early." Jack falls back on the floor with his blanket covering his head. A high pitched laugh came from the figure as she stood in the doorway. Jack and Scott look back up at the figure. It is not Sivanna but someone else. She looks like a bird with a beak, small glasses, and two long feathers hanging down from the side of her head with the rest tied up in a bun. She is wearing a long sleeve shirt and pants but with the same colors and designs as the Elders robes. Jack and Scott look at each other in confusion and another figure enters the room. This time it is Sivanna.

"Hello boys, I told Xolstice to come and wake you. It's time to start training." Jack and Scott moan and both get out of bed and off the floor and walk out the door behind Xolstice and Sivanna.

After a good breakfast of slugberry juice and pancake-like stacks flavored with honey, they all went out to the training grounds. The sit in a circle on the ground and another girl joins them, she is cat-like with ears like a panther, pink fur and purple highlights on the tips of her ears and around her eyes. She is wearing a light purple scarf, a royal blue long sleeve shirt, white pants, and boots that go up to her knees. She is also wearing a belt with two white pockets on either side of her hips. She looks up at Jack and Scott but turns shyly away. Sivanna stands up and speaks.

"Before we begin, I would like to introduce Xolstice's apprentice Suki." Suki looks up and waves shyly.

"Even though she does not speak English well, she will help with your training also. Besides, she will also get a little more practice with her speaking with you two around." Suki begins to blush. Xolstice pats Suki on the shoulder.

"Don't worry Suki; you will be helping them more than anything else through their training especially learning how to get up on time."

Scott and Jack look over with a guilty smile and Scott just lets out a big yawn.

It is about mid-afternoon and after some good stretching and lots of convincing the boys are ready to begin. Sivanna comes up to the boys and with Xolstice and Suki behind her.

"Boys, I need to go finish up with something so you will be starting your training with Xolstice and Suki. Have fun boys." Sivanna walks away back to the village and the boys look up to Xolstice who's smile is gleaming with delight.

"Alrighty boys, who's going to be first?" Jack and Scott look at each other with a little worry in their faces. Xolstice giggles as she bounces a bottle in her hand and Suki with a look of "OH NO" written all over her face. Xolstice throws the bottle at Jack's feet and it breaks. Pink smoke wraps around Jack as he coughs.

"This...COUGH....stuff stinks...COUGH.." Then all of a sudden Jack goes up in a cloud of purple smoke and everyone looks away. Scott looks back to see a grumpy, cute mouse head with elephant size ears, and a goat's body with small wings that is all pink with purple stripes looking back up at him. Scott bursts out laughing and falls to the ground. In a squeaky-pitched voice Jack yells.

"This is soooooo not funny!" He looks at Xolstice. "Why didn't you throw it at Scott?" His cute angry eyes glaring at Xolstice and she just giggles.

"Because it is funnier this way." Jack gets furious and Scott just laughs harder. Suki comes up to Jack and scratches under his chin.

"But you look cute." Scott gets up wiping tears from his eyes and clears his throat and Jack just sits and glares at Xolstice.

"Alrighty Scott now you need to change Jack from a Lucmisst to his normal self." Both Jack and Scott give Xolstice shocked expressions and Jack moves away from Scott and shakes his head.

"WHAT!? SCOTT? Oh No! Naw! Nope! No Way! I might get turned into something else!"

"Well, how else is he going to learn?" Xolstice folds her arms and Suki giggles in the background. Jack swallows hard and sighs.

"Remember you still have to learn too you know." An evil but still cute smile spreads across his face and Scott stops smiling.

"Alrighty Scott now it is time to change Jack back to normal or at least what he usually looks like." Scott and Suki chuckle. Xolstice stands next to Scott and gets ready.

"Ok, to start off you stand in this position." Xolstice is standing with her right foot out , her left hand beside her hip, and her right hand straight out with the palm facing forward. Scott copies her stance and nods his head ready for the next step. Then Xolstice makes both hands into a fist and brings them to her chest and her right foot up next to her left knee. Scott follows. Then Xolstice falls into a lunge position on her right foot, thrusts her right hand out palm first, and bringing her left hand to the side of her head palm facing down and yelling a word in the ancient language. Jack follows but doesn't say the word. Scott looks over at Xolstice whose face is wondering "why didn't you do it?" Xolstice stands back up and clears her throat.

"Maybe I should have taught you the word first. Jack, Scott please come here." They come together and sit down in the grass.

"Well sorry about that. I get carried away sometimes." Jack just rolls his eyes.

"The word to change the person back to normal is *locmi*."

"So it is *lock* and *me* together."

"No it is like *lock* and *pie* put together but the *p* to an *m*." Scott and Jack nod their heads in agreement. So they got back up and Scott tries it once more.

Unfortunately it turned out to be a lot more tries. Sometimes Scott fell doing the moves and other times Jack was turned back to only half of himself, sometimes with big ears, or a goat's tail, or tiny wings on his head instead of his ears. So after a few more tries Jack is finally back to himself. Scott jumps for joy but the joy stops as he hears a crash near his feet. He looks down to see red smoke creeping from the ground up to his face. Then he vanishes into a puff of yellow smoke. In Scott's place sat a scarlet red and darker red striped half squirrel half cat creature. Its golden eyes looking up at everyone then back at itself. Scott grabs his new fluffy tail and plays with his fur. He looks up to see Jack looking back. Scott just smiles with his two large front teeth. Suki comes over and picks Scott up and cradles him in her arms.

"Aww is not cute!" Suki just smiles and Scott looks back in confusion. In a small voice Scott speaks.

"I'm not cute?" his golden eyes getting bigger. Suki just giggles.

"That what me said. Cute!" Scott sighs and snuggles in and Jack is looking on with his mouth hanging open.

"That's unfair! I got turned into this pink monstrosity and he gets turned into a cute squirrel thing." Xolstice laughs and shakes her head.

"It doesn't matter what he gets transformed into, just that he has transformed. He is a Cacirrel. They are well known for those bright golden eyes." Scott looks over at Jack with his big eyes in a curious expression. Jack huffs and turns his head.

Xolstice takes Jack to the side to teach him the moves to perform the spell as Suki and Scott run and chase after one another. Jack looks out to see them laying down laughing in the grass until he feels something hit him in the back of the head. He turns his head to see Xolstice staring at him.

"Pay attention." So they continue to practice until Jack gets it down pat. Then Scott stands in front of Jack as he performs the spell. As with Scott, it took several tries. The one time Jack attempts to get Scott back to normal it didn't turn out to well. He had big golden eyes and everything else was tiny in proportion compared to them. Finally on the last try, Scott is back to normal. So Xolstice sent the boys to go practice so she could go tend to something and for Suki to supervise. The boys and Suki go off to an open patch of grass near the forest to practice. Suki sits on top a rock and watches the boys practice. She would now and then change something and the boys would take turns changing it back. Then the boys stopped and took a small break to relax. Jack lies out in the grass with Scott sitting next to him and Suki comes down to join them.

"So, Suki how long have you been here at this village?" asks Jack. Suki ponders in thought and counts in the air.

"I been here many years. I come here as an apprentice."

"Hmmm, so how old are you?"

"Fifteen." Suki sits back and hugs her knees looking at the boys. Scott turns to face the both of them.

"Your parents must be proud, being an apprentice and all." Suki hugs her knees tighter and looks away and sighs. Scott blushes.

"I'm sorry if that bothered you...I..ah..um..didn't know." Suki stares off to the forest with a sad expression. Jack sits up and faces Suki.

"Did something bad happen to them?" Suki shakes her head *no*.

"So, what happened to them?" Scott bumps Jack in the shoulder and Jack looks back rubbing his shoulder.

"Don't ask that. She may not want to talk about it."

"No, it's not that." Jack and Scott look towards Suki's direction. Xolstice comes walking towards them and kneels down near Suki and hugs her. Suki just closes her eyes.

"She never knew who her parents were or where they are. I first met Suki when she was only just a baby. I found her in a pile of purple flowers wrapped in grey cloth and she was sound asleep. I was still an apprentice then too and didn't know what to do. So I brought her to my teacher and we both raised her here. Then when she was old enough I took her on as my apprentice." Jack and Scott look about guiltily for asking about it. Scott just hangs his head low and Jack just scratches his. Xolstice helps Suki to her feet and motions to the boys to follow.

"Your are done with practice with me today so we are heading back to the village to grab a bite to eat then you two will go continue to practice with Sivanna."

After eating, Jack, Scott, and Sivanna head back to the training grounds. Sivanna passes out the daggers and holds out her dagger in front of the two boys.

"These daggers are not just for show or to defend you. They were made many eons ago by the Goddess Luma Guah. She only gave them to the ones whom the daggers trusted. Then the Goddess taught them, and from then on they are passed on and the new wielders are taught their ancient secrets. So now they have come to you, the newest wielders." Jack and Scott look at their daggers feeling the power course through them.

"Each dagger holds a unique power that only works with its micga word, the tongues of the ancients. For instance, my dagger holds the power of wisdom." The sapphire gem flickers in the late afternoon light. The silver blade gleaming white beams from the sun.

"When you summon your power of the dagger you must point the blade's tip to the object or person you wish to use the power on. Only the wielder of the dagger will know the answer spoken from the dagger. That knowledge you learn can be shared or kept to oneself. During tough or confusing situations I say *helm* and the great goddess shares her wisdom on the situation and helps you decide what to do next. Scott and Jack, your daggers have very unique powers. Scott your dagger holds the Power of Knowledge." Scott looks down at his dagger's garnet gem and watches a faint red light slide across the gem's surface. Scott looks back up.

"Isn't that the same as wisdom?"

"No. Knowledge is knowing what the object is inside and out, the facts about it. Wisdom is using those facts about the objects in play and deciding what is the best choice to deal with those objects." Jack looks down at his deep, purple stone in his dagger and wonders what powers it holds. Before he could ask Sivanna tells him.

"Jack, your dagger holds the Power of Truth. Whatever object you point the dagger's blade to you will learn the true truth of the question you ask of the blade." The boys continue to look over daggers they hold, amazed by the power that resides inside the dagger's soul. Sivanna signals for the boys' attention and takes hold of Scott's dagger and let it lay across both of her hands.

"Scott, your dagger allows you to access knowledge no average person will ever have. What knowledge you learn from this dagger is up to you and how you will use it. Just remember you must ask the question in your mind and not out loud. Also your mind can take in only so much knowledge, so don't overdo it." Jack smirks.

"Well, that won't take too long." Jack laughs at his comment as Scott gets red in the face. He stops laughing when Sivanna gives him a very stern look. Jack just smiles and scratches his head. Sivanna looks back at Scott and continues.

"So to access this power you point your dagger's tip to the object you wish to learn about and say *peyoris.*" Sivanna handed the dagger back to Scott. Scott grabs the dagger by the handle and points the tip to the sky then straight at Jack. Scott breathes in and relaxes. *What is Jack afraid of?* He feels a gentle breeze wrap around his shoulders and a voice whispers in his ear. *His species are afraid of snakes for they are highly allergic to any snake's bite poisonous or not.* Then the breeze left with Scott staring out at a distance then he refocuses at his surroundings. Jack and Sivanna look to see what he might say. Jack crosses his arms and looks straight at Scott.

"Well?" Scott leans his head to the side and scratches the top of his head. Sivanna looks at the both of them.

"Jack, remember that he doesn't have to share with us of what he learned from the goddess. Scott, did she talk to you?"

"Yes, it first felt like a gentle breeze then someone lightly touching my shoulders and whispered in my ear. I felt like I was in some sort of trance." Sivanna smiles and nods.

"That's good then. Now, Jack it is your turn." Jack handed his dagger to Sivanna and lays it upon her hands. She waves her hand over the dagger and sighs then looks up a Jack.

"You must do the same as Scott did but your micga word is *verrass.*" Sivanna hands him back the dagger and without even thinking he points his dagger straight at Scott. He clears his mind and relaxes. *The truth I want to know is how old was Scott when he stopped wetting his bed.* A gentle breeze swirls around him and he could feel a presence behind him. A gentle whisper in his ear makes his ear twitch. *Ten.* Jack's eyes water and he begins to laugh hysterically. Scott's ears lower as he looks in worry.

"What did you ask?" In between gasps for air Jack tells of what he learned.

"You…didn't…stop until you were….TEN!" Jack continues to laugh and Scott's face begins to turn a bright red because he knew what Jack had learned about him. Scott gets up and leaves and Sivanna looks with worry. Sivanna turns to Jack who is lying down.

"If it was something personal it would have been nice of you to not to tell or at least been nicer when saying it." Sivanna got up and went after Scott. Jack watches in disgust as she walks away. *Geez, sorry I hurt mister sensitive,* thought Jack. He falls back down and stares up at the darkening sky. Sivanna meets up with Scott who is sitting behind a tree facing out into the distance. She kneels down and touches his shoulder. Scott just huffs and turns his head away from Sivanna.

"Scott, are you alright?"

"I just need some time to cool off." Sivanna just sighs and rubs his shoulder.

"It's just that it was a personal secret. My older sibling used to make fun of me every time I did. It was very….. hurtful." Scott rests his head on his knees. Sivanna smiles.

"Your secret is safe with me." Scott looks up at Sivanna.

"You promise?"

"Promise." She crosses her fingers and places her other hand on her heart. Scott hugs her and realizes what he is doing and goes back to hugging his knees. He clears his throat.

"Thanks."

Sivanna takes Scott and Jack back to the village to have dinner. Once they have finished they all sat around the fire. Scott, Suki, and Jack are talking amongst themselves. As they talk Suki leans forward and warms her hands by the fire. Out of the darkness, Sivanna and Xolstice come up to the fire and each sit on either side of the kids. Suki taps Jack on the shoulder and the three of them quiet down. Sivanna looks at them with a serious expression.

"I have talked with the other village Elders while you had dinner. They have agreed to let me tell you why you are here and how serious this situation is. This is no longer fun and games. I am going to tell you a story so you three will understand the horrible situation we and Katz are in." Scott, Jack, and Suki grow worrisome.

"I am going to tell you the tale of Nightmare, the Demon of Darkness."

Chapter 8

The children settle down as the night grows dark and the light of the fire reaching for their faces. Sivanna reaches for a pouch near her belt and puts her hand in. With a flick of her wrist the powder flies into the fire. The flames roar to life. They reach for the sky then come back down twirling into the body of the fire. Then the flames swirled open to reveal a faded picture, the colors slowly becoming more and more visible. Sivanna stamps her staff and catches the children's attention.

"Now we begin the story of Nightmare."

The swirling flames reveal a picture of a tiger-like man. He had a strong face yet a scar went across his one eye leaving it white and blind. His other eye's iris is a yellow color with a slit black pupil. He is putting away scrolls from a recently dusted shelf. Radaris is his name. He is the village's head archivist. Radaris checks and organizes the village's scrolls. Each scroll is specifically organized by the time they present in their writing from early beginnings to the present, scrolls on micga and the things around them, from plants to animals. Everything of Azmala's past is here in the scrolls that sit on the shelves around him. Radaris finishes up for the day and gets himself prepared to go talk with the Elders. He has waited for many a year for the Elders to accept him as one of them. The invitation has never come, so Radaris is going to go ask if the Elders if they will allow him to join their ranks. He walks to the main hut in the middle of the village that is next to the fire pit. He pushes a curtain to the side and sees the Elders sitting in a semi-circle on the ground with small cups of tea in front of them. Radaris kneels before them and bows to the ground.

"Elders of the village may I be in your presence?" The Elders nodded to one another accepting Radaris in. Radaris sits up and reclines on his heels.

"Elders I have come to ask a question." He hesitates before the Elders.

"May I become one of you? May I become an Elder? I feel that I am ready." The Elders whisper amongst themselves many with disapproving faces. The head Elder stands and walks towards Radaris and places a hand on his shoulder. A small smile is seen on her old but kind face.

"I am sorry Radaris but we believe you are not yet ready to be an Elder." Radaris stands up and bows his head and leaves. Radaris just walks away from the hut in silence with his head bowed down in disappointment.

Jack, Scott and the others watch as the fire swirls losing the picture and spins into a fast vortex as if fast forwarding to the next part. The fire slowly parts opening to Radaris back in the Archives once more.

Radaris has read every scroll in the archives that he can but a few he is never allowed to set eyes on. Towards the back is a case that seems to always be shadowed in darkness even though the sunlight shines its beams on it. It is the case of Forbidden Scrolls. These scrolls hold ancient secrets of dark and light, good and evil. The only ones that know what these scrolls hold are the Elders. Radaris wants to know what messages, tales, stories, these ancient scrolls hold. Yet he must wait until he is an Elder. As he continues to catalog the scrolls, quiet whispers fill the room. Radaris looks up and moves around the shelves to see no one. Then a whisper calls out to him.

"Radaris."

He looks to see where the voice is coming from and sees it is coming from the Forbidden Scrolls. Radaris shakes his head and denies it and closes up and goes home for the night.

Days pass and nights linger in terror as he awakes every night in fright from an evil, sinister voice calling to him. In his dreams he stands in a dark abyss with no light to be seen in any direction. Then the voice calls out to him.

"*Radaris.*"

Radaris faces the direction the voice is calling him from and sees something in the distance. In a blink of an eye the object levitates before him, a black scroll with faint green lights of energy pulse across its surface. The handles are jagged like crooked hands of bone holding the scroll before him. A lump forms in his stomach as terror fills him. He knows he is forbidden to open the scroll that lies before him. A side of him wishing to run in terror but yet another side yearning to reach out and grab it to unwind the scroll from its twisted grip. He feels a presence behind him.

"*Open the scroll, open it Radaris.*"

Radaris grabs the side of his head and falls to his knees refusing to give in to what he is hearing, over and over again.

"*Open it. Open it! OPEN IT RADARIS!*"

Then Radaris awakes once more, in terror, in the dark, shaking from the nightmare once more.

Nights have passed and Radaris is losing more and more sleep. Every night he fights with this spirit of darkness, refusing to look at the scroll. Then one night before he even closes his eyes he hears a voice.

"Open the scroll Radaris."

This time he freezes in terror. The voice that spoke was his own. The spirit has now taken his own voice and is using it against him. He hears his voice once more.

"Open the scroll."

Radaris sat straight up in bed and balls his fist and stares out into the emptiness in his room.

"NO! I will not open the scroll!"

Then an eerie feeling filled the air as if something is building up and it wasn't good. All of a sudden a force pushes Radaris flat down on the bed and holds him down as if he was strapped to his mattress. He couldn't get free no matter how much he struggled. Then something whispered in his ear, a dark voice mixed with his own speaking to him.

"You will open the scroll. Imagine, the knowledge you will gain."

"No, I will not listen. You are NOT HERE!"

"*What immense knowledge….and power.*"

Radaris gasps at those words the voice tries to put into his head.

"*Yes, power. You may even become an Elder, may be even the head Elder. All you have to do is open the scroll.*"

Then everything stops. Radaris slowly sits up looking about the room. Then in one corner of the room it seems darker than usual. Red eyes appear in the darkness. Then without warning the creature charged him and flew right into him. Radaris is now looking at himself on the bed, his body's head hanging down. Then a fearsome face with red eyes looks back at him with razor sharp teeth and screams.

"RELEASE ME!!!"

Radaris awakens abruptly once again in the middle of the night.

The fire again swirls closed, swirls fast, and opens once more with Radaris walking to the Archives in the dark. Radaris enters the hut. His eyes look past the scrolls in front of him and he stares at the case. He moves towards the back and approaches the case. His eyes filled with a fear-crazed, sleepless gaze. He can no longer bear the sleepless nights being tortured by this spirit. This last night he finally cracked and lost all of his fighting strength. He is now under the spirit's control. Radaris reaches for the scroll he has seen in his dreams countless times. It's green light pulsing in the night. He takes the scroll by its crooked handles and pulls the wrapped parchment open. A green glow comes from the parchment and a great black and evil looking hand rises from the paper and reaches straight into Radaris' chest and grips his heart. Radaris falls to his knees gasping for air and looks up to the scroll floating before him. A voice echoes in the room around him.

"I am the Demon of Darkness. I am to be released from these infernal pages. You are going to go and find the three artifacts that are to release me -- the Soul of an Innocent Child, the Blood of One You Truly Trust, and the Orb of Herahtis. With these artifacts you will bring me into your world."

Radaris stares blankly into the darkness and just muddles words from his mouth.

"I...can't..." A low growl comes from the darkness around him.

"To make sure you will do as I say..."

The scroll rises and darkness swirls around Radaris. The hand that pierces his chest begins to push into his chest and the darkness surrounding Radaris flows into his body. Radaris' body falls lifeless, limp, and cold to the floor. He awakens and stands. He looks at his reflection in window to see nothing but black. Then two red eyes appear and a voice is heard in his head.

"Now, to find the artifacts."

After that night Radaris was never the same. He never went back to the Archives and became distant with fellow villagers. Many have said that when they saw Radaris his white eye would glow red and they would be filled with unknown fear. Before he left the village Radaris lured a young child into the forest and gave the child poisoned berries. The child fell into a deep sleep and Radaris laid the child on her back and crossed her arms over her chest. Before the child's soul left the body he cast a spell and trapped her soul in a vial and placed it into his pocket and left the child. When the parents found her it was most devastating. Nothing like this has ever happened in this peaceful village. They knew the child was murdered by the way she was found. Many began to speculate it is Radaris but no one had proof. Then on another night the head Elder went over to the lake to meditate and ask her goddess what is happening with the village. Her meditation is interrupted by the rustle of leaves behind her. She looks behind her and stops. She could feel a figure standing in front of her and turns her head. She could feel the darkness emanating from its body.

"Why are you here Radaris?"

The figure just stands in silence and then a sudden cold grip takes hold of her and she cannot move. She is brought up and is now face to face with the figure. Radaris looks at her and she gasps.

"Nightmare."

An evil chuckle escapes from Radaris' lips.

"You know what I must do to the one I trusted most?"

She closes her eyes and looks up to the moon.

"My goddess, bring me into your arms gently, save the village, and save Radaris."

Radaris lets out a deep growl and with a swipe of his hand her blood seeps through her skin and she falls limp to the ground. Her blood is gathered into a bottle and placed into his bag. Radaris lays her on her back and crosses her arms on her chest. Tears escape his eyes as he rests his hand on hers. Then a shooting pain courses through his body and he is lifted from the ground and black mass separates from him and floats across from him. He could feel the grip on his body get tighter. Evil laughter comes from the mass.

"*Such pity, a friend killing a friend.Mwahahahaha.*"

Radaris falls to the ground. He gets up and begins to walk away. As he enters the forest he looks back once more at his friend who lies on the shore of the lake, lifeless.

The last artifact lies in a place where no good can survive. Trees lie bare, the ground just dirt and dust, and a silence in the air that no one ever wants to hear. No creature comes through here for their bones will be all that remain of them. Radaris reaches a clearing that looks like something exploded here leaving a scorch mark on the ground forever. In the center of the clearing black smoke crept out of the ground. It swirls slowly up to the colorless sky. When Radaris came close to the center, there lay a small crater, within the crater dark whispers slither out of it. Radaris reaches into the crater and pulls out an orb. He holds the orb out in front of him and the mass separates from him. It floats around the orb and chuckles.

"Finally, the Orb of Herahtis."

The mass disappears and forms in front of Radaris.

"Take all three artifacts to the tallest point in Azmala and perform the incantation and release me."

Radaris looks at the orb and ponders. Then a force grabs his throat. The spirit floats in front of him.

"NOW!"

Radaris climbs the highest hill in Azmala. He looks over the edge to see how far the cliff goes down and sees tiny rocks at the bottom. Radaris hears a voice in his head.

"Begin the incantation."

Radaris stands facing the cliff and holds the three artifacts in his hands over the cliff's edge. He closes his eyes and drops the artifacts. He takes his staff and holds it in front of him. He chants the incantation.

"Creature of the deepest darkness, the demon of torture, the heartless, the soulless knight, I call to you now to do my darkest bidding. I say rise, RISE NIGHTMARE, DEMON OF DARKNESS!"

The clouds darken and swirl above the cliff. Wind begins to howl and whip through the trees. Screams and cries of fear fill the air. The air becomes frigid and cold and all life silenced. The ground begins to rumble and shake. The rocks at the bottom of the cliff part ways letting out an eerie green glow that gets brighter and brighter as the cracks widen. Wisps of dark smog seep through the cracks and begin to gather in an orb shape just a few feet from the cliff's drop. It continues to grow as more and more wisps fly through the air. Then the dark orb stretches and grows forming a being. The body stretches towards the opening in the earth and widens up to pointed shoulders and a round head forms with a hat shape upon it. Then it stops, it all stops. A terrible sound came from the being. It became louder and turned into maniacal laughter. The head rises up to reveal bright glowing red eyes and razor sharp teeth. Its expression is of pure evil and hate. The hat upon its head too had glaring red eyes and razor sharp teeth. The creature's arms reached for the sky and purple lightning flashes across the horizon as thunder rolls.

"YES! I AM FREE! MWAHAHAHAHAHA! I am Nightmare, Demon of Darkness!"

Radaris looks up at Nightmare.

"Nightmare you are under my control. I summoned you!"

Nightmare leans over Radaris and glares at him.

"You cannot control me. I am the one controlling you, hmmmm, now what to do with you."

Nightmare stands straight and raises a hand over Radaris and shadows him. A great pulse of energy shoots out of Nightmare's hand directly into Radaris. Radaris can feel pain in every part of his body. It feels like he is going to explode and he cries out in pain. Then he lies limp on the ground and Nightmare chuckles.

"You are better off dead. And now, I'll use your body to my advantage."

Nightmare swipes his hand across Radaris' body and black fog surrounds him. Cracking and breaking sounds come from the body as it is consumed by the black fog. Then a low growl emanates from the fog and a creature jumps out. It is a creature of darkness and minion of Nightmare's. It is a Nightling. It's body sunken showing it's pointed shoulders, hips, and joints. It has long claws and two long fangs coming from its mouth and two bent horns protruding from the top of its head and stretching back. It has a long tail with a pointed dagger tip. The Nightling is a deep midnight blue with deep purple stripes and Nightmare's brand on the top of its hands, chest, and forehead. The Nightling screeches into the night.

"Go and destroy the village and break the bloodline to the moon goddess."

The Nightling charges through the forest and sneaks into the village quietly. It jumps in front of the fire pit in the middle of the village and scares the people nearby. It stands up and its hands pulse with green energy that it shoots at the fire pit causing a great explosion. Then it starts shooting the green energy at homes, using it claws to scratch and tear at people, and using its poison tipped tail to paralyze its victims. It runs through the village burning homes, killing everyone, destroying lives. It sets the Archives into flames and people nearby watch as their history burn to ashes. The Nightling reaches a house near the edge of the village and stands before it. Its hands pulse and glow, then with all its might it blows green fire and sets the house ablaze. It stands and growls in wait to hear screams of the family and hears nothing. Then it hears a child's cry. It turns around to see the family fleeing from the house. The Nightling cries out and chases after the family. The father nods to his wife and he turns to face the Nightling. He pulls out his sword and stands ready for it. The Nightling stops and paces around the man, the man's heart pounding in his chest waiting for it to attack. Then the creature disappears. Before he could act the Nightling jumps up from behind and bites his neck. The man yells and his wife turns to look with tears in her eyes, her child crying in her arms. She continues to run as she hears the Nightling nearing her. She turns a corner and the Nightling throws them both to the ground. The mother places her child under a fallen tree branch near them and tells her to be quiet. The child, with tears in her eyes, watches as her mother walks away and begins to whimper. The mother takes the crystal from her necklace and places it in her dagger and it transforms into a mystical sword, a sword of pure light. She lashes left and right at the Nightling and it dodges every attack. Then she hits it square across the chest and it screams in pain. It lunges at her and lands on her on the ground. She could not move and the Nightling lifts its tail revealing the tip that glows red. As the tip drags across her arm, the Nightling is knocked off. She looks up to see an older woman standing there with her staff in hand. She swings it above her head and hits the Nightling with a ball of light and sends it flying. It crashes to the ground and runs off. The woman walks over to her daughter and holds her hand. Her daughter looks up at her.

"Elder Sivanna, can you please bring my daughter to me."

Sivanna stands up and walks over to the crying child and picks her up. She cradles her in her arms and then sits next to her mother. The mother reaches out her hand to her child.

"My child, I bless you with the Gift of the Goddess Luma Guah. May she protect you always." She places the crystal from her necklace into her child's hand and falls never to wake again. Sivanna takes the crying child back to the other villagers and Elders and leaves the child with a fellow Elder. Then Sivanna and five other Elders walk into the forest to face the terror destroying their village.

The Nightling came back crawling up the hill to Nightmare. Disgusted with the Nightling's failure to destroy the bloodline, he throws it to the ground which in turn changes its body back to Radaris'. Nightmare knows the Elders are coming so he will use Radaris' body for one more task.

The Elders emerge from the forest, at the bottom of the hill where Nightmare looms over. At the top of the hill a figure stands. Sivanna realizes who it was.

"Fellow Elders, Radaris, now known as the Wizard of Dark, has brought back a darkness once sealed away by the goddess herself. Now we ourselves must do the same."

The Elders approach the hill. One of the Elders cries out.

"Wizard of Dark why have you done this to our land? Why are you so displeased?"

Radaris turns to face the Elders and an evil laughter responds to her question.

"OUR land? So foolish you are! This land is mine and so is its power. I will be ultimate. I WILL BECOME SUPREME RULER OF ALL! MWAAHAHAHAHAHAHA!"

The Elders form a circle around the Wizard of Dark and Nightmare. They begin to chant and a bright white light blinds all who see. Then when the light clears, the Wizard of Dark and Nightmare have vanished. The clouds part and the light of the moon shines once more.

The fire swirls down into the pit and settles back down into a normal fire, quietly crackling in the night. The children sit back and realize what a truly dangerous situation they are in. Xolstice gets up and puts out the fire. Sivanna looks toward the children.

"It is now time to rest and you may ask your questions in the morning. Good night children, and let the goddess protect you."

They parted ways and went back to their beds, their heads full of questions. Scott and Jack say good night to Suki, Xolstice, and Sivanna. As the boys get tucked in for the night Scott sits up in bed and hugs his knees.

"Jack."

"Yeah, Scott?"

"Can we leave a light on tonight? To..um..ah..in case I need a glass of water, and don't trip over anything."

"Fine." Jack turns and faces the wall away from Scott. He sighs realizing what is really happening around him.

"Jack?"

"Yes Scott?"

"What did we get ourselves into?"

Jack looks towards Scott's direction without turning over then back at the wall. He closes his eyes waiting to see what the next day may bring.

Chapter 9

Many cups of tea later, Katz's voice is returned to normal but she must remain quiet in the presence of Nightmare and Hat. Katz is now in the library of the old castle. Massive shelves line the walls from top to bottom. As you enter the library to the right is a metal spiral staircase that leads up to a landing where it stretches across the middle of the shelves all the way around. Rolling ladders line the lower shelves and three chairs sit in a triangle like shape spread far apart. But the most eye catching part of the library is the window seat where you can sit and read and look out the window. The seat is long enough for two people to sit and lay out their legs across the cushioned surface. Pillows line the bottom of the window and a single book lies on top of one of the pillows. Yet the most beautiful part is the stained glass design along the edge of the window. A big reddish-pink rose sits up towards the top in the middle of the window. Long, slender vines fall from its sides down the outer edges of the window with smaller roses and buds intertwined into the vines. Two white doves sit on either side of the big rose, forever in flight. The sight of the window fills Katz's heart with joy. The beauty of it is so magnificent. *This place would be such a wonderful place to read,* thought Katz but she is not here to read, she is here to clean. So she takes out a feather duster and starts dusting the shelves and books. As she looks closer at the books on the shelves she could see that each and every one of them look like they were never touched by time. They were a little dusty but in the utmost condition. Katz walks down the shelf with her fingers sliding across each book's binding. They seem to call out to her asking her to pick them up and read the stories that hide within them. Katz turns with a start when she hears the door slam shut behind her.

"I see you like the library."

It is Vladmir. He walks over to one of the chairs and takes the white sheet off and shakes off the dust, folds it, and lays it across the back of the chair. Vladmir sits down, crosses his feet, and holds his hands together with only the fingertips touching just in front of his chest. He looks up at Katz and gestures to Katz to keep cleaning. Katz pouts at him, crosses her arms, and turns to the shelves and starts cleaning. A silence lingers for a moment between them and Katz turns around.

"How about we play the 20 question game?"

"The what?"

"The 20 question game, since I don't know much about you it's a fun way to learn about someone. I ask ten questions and you ask ten questions, just don't ask any stupid, crazy, or super personal questions."

"Ok. You go first." Vladmir sits in his chair watching Katz for the first question. Katz ponders for a moment bouncing the duster in her hand. Then a question comes to mind.

"What is your favorite color and why?"

Vladmir ponders for a moment and answers.

"Midnight blue because it reminds me of the night sky and its silent beauty. Now for my question, what is your favorite color and why?"

Katz just smiles.

"My favorite color is red because it represents so many things. Like warmth, cheer…" She sighs. "And love."

Katz looks up at the stained glass rose and watches as the moon's glow shines through its translucent frame. She continues to look out the window.

"What is your favorite food?" Katz hears rustling above her and she looks up.

"I don't have one in particular just as long as it is not crawling across my plate."

Vladmir ruffles through the pages of a book as Katz looks at him in disbelief.

"Weren't you just sitting down here in that chair?"

Katz points to the chair while looking back up at Vladmir. He looks out the corner of his eye while holding the book open in his hand.

"Is that your next question?"

Vladmir looks back down at the book and chuckles as Katz looks up at him red in the face and confused. She shakes her head.

"No."

Vladmir walks down the spiral staircase while looking in the book.

"So, then what is your favorite food?"

Katz giggles at the thought. "Cake."

Katz licks her lips as the thought crosses her mind.

"So, Vladmir, what do you mostly dislike?"

Vladmir is now sitting back in the chair with the book at his lap. He looks up at Katz then hides behind the book with a sickening look.

"Garlic."

"Really? It is such a tasty ingredient to add to dishes. Like..."

As she mentions different dishes Vladmir pulls the book closer to his face each time she mentions garlic. Then Katz is spooked by the loud slam of the book closing in Vladmir's hand. He sits the book on his lap and places a hand underneath his chin and smiles.

"What do you dislike the most?"

Katz shivers at the thought and looks away.

"Water."

Katz walks over to another chair and pulls it towards Vladmir's chair so that she is sitting off to the side of him. She plops her butt down into the chair and dust flies into the air. Katz coughs and waves the dust away from her face.

"So, have you ever traveled?"

"Yes but not too far."

Then a wonderful question came to Vladmir's mind.

"Do you like music?"

"Ah yes. I love music very much. What type of music do you like?"

"Violin music. I believe it's music from the soul."

When Vladmir looks up at Katz he could see her just looking about the library, at all the books sitting on the shelves.

"What type of books do you like to read?"

Katz looks down at her twiddling thumbs and sighs.

"I'm not much of a big reader, but I'll read once in a while. Hey, did you read all of these books?"

Katz looks amongst the books once more. Vladmir looks away and sighs.

"Yes, I have a lot of spare time. Some of these books I have read more than once. Which reminds me, how did you come upon this castle?"

"Well, to make it short. My friends, Jack and Scott, and I were trick or treating and we were just going for a walk after dinner. Jack decided to tell an old tale, a legend of this old castle. I was afraid at first but..."

Katz got up and started pacing with anger written all over her face.

"But noooo! Jack and Scott thought I was a scaredy cat and wouldn't go anywhere near the castle even if it was there, which I find out it is. We came in, we investigated, and got scared by something in the castle. We tried to escape but... I didn't."

Katz sits back down and sinks into the chair. She looks towards the window longing for home and away from this dreadful place. Then a question came to her mind.

"Vladmir, how long have you been here, in this castle?"

Vladmir looks down and crosses his arms.

"For far too long but who are your friends, Jack and Scott?"

Katz leans on the arm of the chair with her head in her hand and smiles.

"They are my friends, even though they can be a real pain sometimes. Jack is a typical wolf that is sometimes too full of himself, yet he was always there for me. Scott on the other hand is so different from Jack. He is the goofiest raccoon you would ever meet. He can always find a way to make you smile, especially when his face is covered in gravy."

Katz smiles and giggles at the thought of her friends. Then a solemn look is seen on her face.

"I do miss them very much though. Well, what about you? Do you do anything else besides read all day?"

"Eh, not much really. I drink tea, read books, play my violin, draw or just sit on my butt all day and do nothing."

Katz smiles and giggles.

"So, where do you come from Katz? Your home?"

"I come from Old Oak town just south of Old Oak City."

Katz realizes that Vladmir is no longer in the chair but back up on the landing looking through the books once more. Katz stands up in a huff all fed up.

"How do you get around the castle so fast?"

She stands with her arms down to her sides waiting for an answer. Vladmir just chuckles as he leaves through a book.

"Well, if I told you it won't be a secret anymore, would it?"

Vladmir looks down at Katz who is giving the angry pouty face again and he just laughs quietly to himself.

"So, do you like anything about this castle?"

Katz is down by the shelves dusting once more.

'Well, there are a few good things about the castle. I wish I could have seen it in its hey days. It was probably so beautiful like that garden out in the court yard. Is that your garden?"

"Yes. What do like about the garden?"

"Those beautiful glowing flowers around the fountain, they remind me of light of the moon when it is full on a clear night. Every time I clean in the foyer or at the top of the stairs and when that stupid Hat is not there, I just like to just stare at its beauty. It is just so lovely like it was made with love."

Katz just stares off into space thinking about the garden and Vladmir hides in his book with sadness in his face. Then Vladmir notices something. Katz looks up from her cleaning stuff.

"What is that smell? It smells like something is burning."

Vladmir drops the book, runs down the stairs, and slams the doors open and runs down the hall.

"Vladmir, WAIT!!!"

Katz runs after Vladmir down the hall with the burning smell becoming stronger. She turns the corner watching Vladmir bang on the main foyer window leading to the garden. Katz runs up next to Vladmir whose face is full of distraught. She turns her head and looks out the window. She watches in fear as the orange glow lights up her face. Down from the window they stand in front of, every blade of grass, every petal, every last one burning. The fire roars up the sides of the walls like a terrible creature trying to escape. Its flame tipped fingers reaching for the top of the walls, its body consuming the garden. Katz noticed the roses that lined the fountain beginning to curl as they char and blacken losing the color they used to hold. The garden dies with silent screams as the laughter of the crackling fire continues. Katz looks back at Vladmir who continues to watch the flames. He closes his eyes and grinds his teeth then he screams.

"NOOOOOOOOOOOOOOOO!!!!!!"

Vladmir slams both of his fists against the window. He hit so hard that the glass should have broke but with each hit the glass heals. Then they both feel a cold presence come up from behind them. They both turn. Katz gasps as Vladmir stares straight into the eyes of Nightmare.

"I warned you not to interfere with my plans. Now your garden burns. It will burn to a lifeless field of ash."

Vladmir just glares and breathes deep rushed breaths. He clenches his fists.

"We made that garden together! I promised her that I would keep it like she wanted it to!"

"My, a promise not well kept is it now?"

Nightmare smiles back with his sharp teeth gleaming in the fire's light. Vladmir lunges forward.

"NIGHTMARE!!!"

Before even Vladmir could hit Nightmare, he grips him by the throat and lifts him off the ground. Nightmare holds Vladmir to his face.

"Do you think I would truly leave you alone? Even though he is not in plain sight my minion watches you. He saw everything that you have been doing."

Vladmir's expression changes into a shocked expression. Hat plops out from behind Nightmare smiling sarcastically.

"Every move, every breath, he was watching. Now that you have continued to disobey me you shall stand with me and watch your garden burn."

A force takes control of Vladmir and makes him walk towards the window and makes him face out the window. No matter how much he fights, the force keeps his eyes straight out the window at the flames. Nightmare looms over next to him. Katz watches them as the glow of the orange light illuminates the outline of their bodies. She clenches her fist and looks up at Nightmare. She runs towards him.

"NIGHTMARE!"

As she reaches the window he disappears and before she could act a force takes hold of her and shrouds her in a dark mist. She can feel it squeezing tighter and tighter. Katz gasps for air as Nightmare's face appears from the darkness. An evil chuckle rang in the darkness. Katz gasps her last breath and faints. Then Nightmare throws Katz through the window and down into the fire. She lays there lifelessly next to the wall of the fountain, the flames fingers flickering by her face. Vladmir stands there not able to move his body, his arms down by his side, and his feet together as the heat of the fire blows past him. He looks angrily out into the flames.

"She had nothing to do with this Nightmare."

Nightmare came up next to Vladmir.

"Yes she did. More than you think."

Nightmare laughs manically as he disappears into the darkness. Vladmir still stands there still not being able to move. He watches as the flames creep closer to Katz. Then straight in front of him at a distance a black swirling cloud floats above the fire. Vladmir watches both Katz and the cloud. All of a sudden the cloud shoots towards Vladmir and straight into him. He falls to the ground feeling his body painfully get cold and making it harder to breathe. He turns to see if he can see Katz and Nightmare's face appears out of nowhere.

"NOW WATCH HER DIE!"

Vladmir tries to get up but his body refuses. Every bone in his body ached in pain. He manages to lift his head up enough to see Katz with the flames now very close to her. He falls back to the ground with the feeling a helplessness overwhelming him. With what strength he could muster he pulls himself to the edge and rolls over. He falls to the hard ground where soft grass used to grow. He looks out towards the fountain across the scorched ground looking for Katz. His body is still freezing so he moves over towards a burning bush to see if that warms his body. He lays there coughing as the smoke billows around him. Then all of a sudden the coldness went away and he is able to get up. As he lifts himself, he dusts the ash off of his clothes and looks around for Katz. He spots her near the fountain lying motionless. Vladmir quickly dodges the fire's flames and heads towards Katz.

From a window looking over the garden from the right side a figure stands. He watches as Vladmir inches closer to the lifeless girl. The glowing light of the flames reflect in the window as its fiery fingers reach for the window's edge. The figure stands and watches as Vladmir picks up Katz caringly. He holds her tight as he takes the door to exit the burning garden. He looks back to see his sweet memories swept away by the heat of the fire. Ashes swim pass his face as if the spirit of the garden gives him a kiss goodbye. As Vladmir enters the doorway the figure in the window takes a glowing orb with a purple-black mist surrounding it. It holds it out in front of him and smiles. Its dagger-like fingertips grip and gouge into the orb piercing its surface. Across the way it watches as Vladmir falls to his knees.

A sharp pain courses through his heart. He breathes in sharply and crawls further into the doorway on his knees into the kitchen. Another wave of shooting pain courses his body and he drops Katz in front of him and he falls gripping his chest. They both lie motionless for a moment and Katz stirs. Her eyelids flutter open to see Vladmir lying across from her. She gets up and rubs the back of head. She reaches over to Vladmir.

"Vladmir? Vladmir are you ok? Vladmir?!"

Katz takes his arm and turns him over. Vladmir falls onto his back with one hand still gripping his chest. Vladmir breathes in sharply as if deeply in pain and Katz notices something. Beneath Vladmir's gloved hand that is gripping his chest a red stain began to appear. Katz gasps and places her hands over her mouth as tears came to her eyes. Vladmir is bleeding and bad. Vladmir cringes as wave upon wave of pain shoots through him, every fiber of his body radiating pain. Vladmir tries to get up and stumbles. Katz moves over to Vladmir where his head is now laying on her lap. She reaches out her hands and holds Vladmir's free hand. Vladmir opens his eyes to see Katz's face wet with tears. In his shaking hand he can feel hers holding on tight. Between each gasp of pain he speaks.

"Katz.....there's something I need to tell....you"

She looks down.

"Please Vladmir don't, your hurt."

"No. I..... must. I should..have.. told you sooner. When..we..first met."

Vladmir curls up as a powerful wave of pain surges his body. He clamps down on his teeth and groans. Then he lies back down. Nightmare watching from the window listens to the conversation and realizes what is going on. He takes the orb in his hand and squeezes to almost where his fingertips are touching inside the orb. Vladmir yells out in extreme pain and his eyes close and he falls. Katz watches his lifeless body hoping for any movement. Nothing. She gently lays his head on the ground and moves his hand from his chest. Holding back her tears she began with only what she could have thought of at the moment, CPR. Katz presses down on his chest three times, blows air into his lungs, and listens. She tries again and still nothing. She sat back on her knees feeling hopeless. Then she just falls apart. She begins to cry uncontrollably. The only friend she had in this dark time is now gone.

Nightmare, who is still watching, motions to Hat to retrieve a vial from the shelf. Nightmare pops the cork and drops two white drops of liquid onto the orb. As he held the vial in his hand the orb began to pulsate once more.

"Pathetic."

He looks back towards the kitchen door and sees movement.

Katz looks up to hear Vladmir moan quietly. She sees Vladmir's chest come up then down slowly. His hand slowly grips his chest and he looks over to Katz.

"I'm sorry."

A black-grayish mist envelopes them both and Katz loses sight of Vladmir. Katz reaches out and realizes she is back in her room, back with the rusty boiler. She slowly lies down and cries into the night.

Down in a dark room where a fireplace lies cold, a figure lays upon the couch. It is Vladmir. He just lays motionless as he waits for the pain to subside. He closes his eyes and started to drift off to sleep. Then a sound awakens him. A sound he hasn't heard in a long time. THUMP, THUMP went the sound. He opens his eyes. He sits up slowly on the couch to see a figure near the door. It is Nightmare. He floats there with a snarly smile and holding out something. He disappears and the sound gets louder. He reappears in front of Vladmir holding the orb in front of him. Vladmir watches as the orb pulsates with the beating sound of a heart. Nightmare grips the orb only slightly and Vladmir grips his chest.

"This will be the last time you will ever hear or see your heart."

As Nightmare disappears into the darkness his evil laughter and his words are left to ravage the room and torture Vladmir for the rest of the night.

Chapter 10

In the dew of the warm morning, the birds sing and the creatures skitter across the grass. The sun sits on the edge of the horizon rising slowly to the sky. Everything is at peace but in the village everyone is awake and running to prepare, yet two still lie in their beds. These two are very tired from a restless night of sleep. The danger they now know haunted them in their sleep, worried about what is yet to come. A soft knock is heard at the door to their room. The door opens to Suki looking to see the two boys sleeping in messy beds. She walks over in between the two beds.

"Jack, Scott, time come out of bed. Morning." said Suki softly. The boys do not move. Suki goes over to Jack and gently shakes his shoulder.

"Jack, wake up, morning."

Jack moans and turns over to see Suki sitting on the edge of the bed looking at him curiously. He nods his head and Suki smiles and leaves. Jack sits up, stretches, and yawns. He looks over at Scott who is snoring up a storm. He picks up his pillow and tosses it at Scott's face. Scott stops snoring and moans.

"Hey, wake up!"

Scott sits up and stretches and throws the pillow back at Jack and misses.

"You could have been gentler waking me up you know."

They get up, get ready for the day, and head out the door.

Xolstice, Suki, Jack, and Scott are back out in the training grounds. Next to Xolstice are four bags. Xolstice stands in front of Jack, Scott, and Suki.

"Alrighty, before we start our lesson for the day, we need to go find some ingredients. So each of you have a bag in which you will gather herbs and other plants. I will not tell you what plants or herbs you need to get but you will pick and take what you believe we can use in a potion. Suki and Jack will go together and Scott and I will team up. Now let's grab our bags and shove off."

They each grab a bag and head into the forest.

Jack and Suki come up to a small clearing where a small pond shines in the sun. Suki is busy picking mushrooms and Jack goes up to the lake and looks amongst the plants there. He picks a red flower with blue leaves, a brown three-leaf clover, and another that caught his eye. It is a pale blue and is shaped like a paper lantern with white strings popping out from the top. Then they both continue into the forest until they come upon a big open clearing with few trees. Suki went off on her own, while Jack scouts for more interesting plants. He picks one that looks like a miniature sunflower, a purple spike ball, and yet another interesting one. It looks like a simple blade of grass but it blooms open revealing beautiful white and pink petals and deep inside the petals a clear liquid settles at the bottom. When he picks the flower, it closes up only looking like a blade of grass. Jack and Suki then continue on once more back into the forest.

Scott and Xolstice enter the forest and stop in crowded spot of trees and different types of fungus growing everywhere. Xolstice is picking and throwing plants and fungus either in her bag or behind her. Scott decides to keep his distance and starts looking around. He picks up a blue mushroom, a piece of blue and green moss off a tree and finds a mushroom with a white net-like top and a green stem.   Then they walk up near a lake where very colorful fish swim in the water. Xolstice pushes away tall weeds and heads behind them. Scott spots a fish that is a florescent green color and follows it. Scott walks up the bank, jumps across a couple of stones and then the fish disappears amongst some tall grass growing out of the water. He looks up and sees the top of the grass. Hidden amongst the grass is a tall, beautiful purple flower. The petals are long and slender with streak of black down the middle. Two little blue strings stand straight up in the middle of the petals. Scott picks up the flower from the water and spots the fish.

"Thanks for the flower," said Scott as he tilted the flower in the fish's direction. Scott wonders farther into the forest. The sun peeks in and out of the tops of the trees to shine on the forest floor. As he walks passed a couple of trees he spots a big rock in the middle of the small opening. It looks like it has been sitting there for many years, covered in moss and vines of plants growing from its cracks. Scott walks around the rock and spots a small white flower. As he gets closer he notices a purple dot in the very center.

"Scott? Scott where are you?" calls Xolstice.

Scott quickly picks the flower and places it in his bag and meets up with Xolstice.

Now they are back at the training grounds sitting together, empting their bags. Xolstice went down the line and Jack is first.

"This red flower that you found doesn't do much but its leaves can help someone with a terrible cough. Good. This brown three-leaf clover is a fun one. If you ever eat something poisonous you eat this to puke it back up."

Jack looks at the brown plant disgustingly.

"Geez what did the plant ever do to you? Well, anyways. This blue lantern flower helps in a special healing potion for medium grade wounds like deep cuts and gouges. This little purple spike ball is used for potions to make quick escapes. It produces a liquid, which when heated, produces a big cloud of smoke."

Then she picks up the miniature sunflower and places next to Jack's ear.

"This flower doesn't do anything for a potion but it does look nice on you."

Jack pulls the flower from his ear and tosses it aside as Xolstice giggles at him. Then Xolstice holds up the flower that looks like a blade of grass. Scott just laughs.

"You picked a blade of grass! That won't do anything! Ha Ha!!"

Xolstice gives him a sarcastic look.

"Well, he picked the one of the more difficult flowers to find."

Xolstice gently squeezes the sides exposing the white and pink petals. Scott's jaw drops.

"This flower helps with burns. The clear liquid inside its petals can be placed on any type of burn and heals it instantly."

Xolstice goes over Suki's plants and then goes in front of Scott's collection. She picks up the blue mushroom and chuckles.

"Ah, I used these many of times. If you ever want to tease someone for a day just mix this into their food. It will give them the hiccups all day. As for this green and blue moss this helps with those with severe allergic reactions to things. Once you dry it out, just one good blow in the face with the powder they are back to normal."

Then Xolstice picks up the mushroom with the white-net top and green stem.

"This little bugger gives you the most nasty stomach cramps you'll ever have. A child ate this one day and boy she was one unhappy camper."

The purple flower is next.

"My, this one is a little angel if processed correctly. If not processed correctly you'll have a nasty red rash all over your body, if processed correctly it acts as a medicine, if taken daily, will help those with terrible illnesses over time to get better."

Then she picks up the little white flower. She has a worried look on her face.

"Scott, where did you find this flower?"

"I found it on a big rock that was all covered in moss and vines."

"Ah. This flower, when made with many, is a lethal poison if not taken care of quickly. It starts with a fever and a purple mark appears on your right palm, then you become violently ill and are unable to eat and drink. If this is not taken care of you will eventually fall into a deep sleep and not awaken."

Suki, Jack, and Scott look at each other with worry. A spark of light takes place of the white flower and the smoke clears leaving no flower behind. Scott looks down at his feet.

"Sorry, I didn't know it was a *bad* flower."

Xolstice comes over and places her hands on his shoulders.

"That's what learning is about. Now you know that you must stay away from that flower. That goes for you two also."

Suki, Jack, and Scott all nod their heads. Xolstice takes a small dagger from her belt and pricks her finger and shows it to them.

"Now your lesson for today is all about healing. We will start out simple. To heal any wound you put your hand above the wound and say *yileese.*"

As she said the word the prick on her finger heals like it was never there. She walks up to Scott and pricks her finger and holds it out to him.

"Heal it."

Scott looks at Xolstice and then at her finger. He places his hand just above her finger.

"Yileese."

When Scott removes his hand he is very glad to see that Xolstice's finger is healed and not disfigured or something. Xolstice pricks her finger again and brings it before Jack.

"Your turn."

Jack looks down at her finger, places his hand over her finger, and speaks.

"Yileese."

And again her finger is healed. Then Xolstice takes her dagger once more and makes a small slice across her arm about four inches in length. She went up to Scott once more.

"Heal."

"Yileese."

Yet this time even though she is healed, Scott began to feel a little weak. He puts his hand to his head. Xolstice looks down at him.

"You will be all right."

Xolstice cuts her arm once more about the same length and presents to Jack.

"Heal."

"Yileese."

As the same with Scott, Jack became a little weak. Xolstice rolls down her sleeve.

"As you now know, when you heal someone, it takes energy from you. The bigger the wound the more energy you need. You will eventually become stronger and be able to know what amount of energy you'll need; it will vary depending on the severity. But, before I do the next one are you sure you will be alright with it?"

Scott and Jack look at Xolstice with great worry on their faces. Scott looks up at Xolstice.

"What exactly are you going to do?"

Xolstice smiles and pulls out here dagger.

"Don't worry I have done this many times before and even to Suki."

The boys look over at Suki who is just smiling away. Xolstice takes her dagger and stabs herself in her left thigh and pulls the dagger back out. The boys look in horror with their jaws to the floor. Scott's knees begin to wobble and then he just falls, passed out on the ground. Jack runs over to Scott to see if he is okay and Suki tends to Xolstice. Suki and Xolstice come over to check up on the boys. Scott opens his eyes to see the three of them staring back down at him.

"I passed out didn't I?"

Jack just smiles.

"Yes you did. Ha Ha."

"Sorry. I just freak out when I see that happen. My body doesn't know how to react and just shuts down. "

Suki kneels down by Scott.

"Why faint? Was it the sight of blood?"

Scott shakes his head.

"No. I believe it is from when I was exposed to a scary movie at a young age. But it was by accident though!"

Suki stands up to make room for Xolstice as she kneels down to be able to talk to Scott.

"You should have told me. Anyways, are you okay for me to continue teaching?"

"Yes, I'll be fine just next time give me a chance to tell you."

Jack helps Scott to his feet and Scott dusts off. Suki walks up next to Xolstice and Xolstice pulls out her dagger once more.

"So, are you okay for me to continue?"

"Yes."

Xolstice takes her dagger once more and stabs her thigh. She falls to the ground and Suki comes and takes Jack over to Xolstice. He heals her but falls to his knees with the energy taken from him. Now it is Scott's turn. Xolstice stabs herself once more and Suki brings Scott over. With a shaking hand, he places his hand over her wound.

"Yileese."

He watches as her wound heals but then it starts to open again. Scott places his hand over once more wobbling from the energy already taken from him but another hand lays on top of his. He looks over to see Suki smiling.

"It okay."

Suki closes her eyes and her hand begins to glow. Scott can feel the energy flow back into him in a gentle cool current. With both hands over Xolstice they both speak.

"Yileese."

Xolstice's wound closes up and for good this time. They all breathe a sigh of relief. Xolstice stands up and dusts herself off. She gives a thumbs up to Scott who smiles and Suki giggles.

"You two are learning quite fast. That's good."

They turn around to see Sivanna walking towards them. She takes hold of Xolstice's hand and nods thanking her for her time to train the boys. Xolstice and Suki head off back to the village. Sivanna places the box she is carrying with her on the ground and takes off her robe. She is now wearing a simple outfit of a shirt and pants with similar colors and design as her robe. Around her waist is a belt with the dagger in its holder. Sivanna opens the box and pulls out two more belts similar to hers. She gives them to the boys. Then she returns to the box and takes out a smaller box. It is the decorative box she received from Elder Niah. She opens the box and the boys reach in grabbing their daggers. They both place their daggers into their holders.

"Now that you have some basic micga under your belt, now it's time to begin melee combat training. But before we start I need to see what you can do."

She looks over at Scott.

"Attack me."

Both Jack and Scott look at each other with confused looks. Scott looks back at Sivanna and lunges at her. He runs with the dagger's tip point up in his hand. As he begins to strike Sivanna moves out of the way, hits his arm at the elbow causing him to drop his dagger. Then she wraps her arm around his neck and with her other hand she places the dagger beneath his chin. Sivanna lets go of Scott. He stands up and rubs his neck.

"Scott, you need to be serious about this. Attack me like you are in real danger. Act like I am your worst enemy. So again, attack me."

Sivanna tosses Scott his dagger and he catches it. He runs towards Sivanna with the dagger at his side. Sivanna strikes down at him and Scott dodges and brings his dagger to the back of Sivanna's neck. She reaches back and blocks it. Scott comes back around in a spin and knocks Sivanna's legs from underneath her and she falls on her back. Scott comes to strike down and Sivanna blocks his attack again. She grabs him by his wrist that is holding the dagger and pulls him down just above her dagger just barely touching his chest. Sivanna and Scott lock eyes and pant heavily. Sivanna smiles and lets go. Scott backs off and helps Sivanna up.

"Now that's an attack. You need a little work but still good. Now Jack show me what you can do."

Scott went off to the side and sits down in the grass to relax. Sivanna and Jack pace face to face in a circle waiting for who will make the first move. Jack lunges at her with his dagger pointed right at her. Sivanna dodges his attack and as he comes by she hits him square in his back causing him to fall. Jack gets to his knees facing away from Sivanna. He quickly stands up and attacks Sivanna again. Once again Sivanna knocks him down. As Jack stands back up, a dark anger releases in him. He turns and watches Sivanna as the walk in a circle once more. Sivanna lunges forward and Jack jumps over Sivanna and turns and slices Sivanna across her back. Sivanna stands up touching her back and looks at her hand, there is blood. Scott stands up. In anger Jack screams and charges Sivanna once more. Sivanna stands to defend his attack until Scott flies into Jack and knocks him off to the side. Both of their daggers go flying in either direction. Scott is on top of Jack and he holds him down by his shoulders.

"Jack?! What are you doing? You could have really hurt her!"

Jack looks back up with anger and tries to wriggle free. Scott firmly holds Jack down not allowing him not to move an inch.

"Jack, she is just training us! You need to stop! Control your anger!!"

Jack closes his eyes and clenches his fists. He starts to breathe in fast at first but begins to breathe in slower. Scott gently got off of Jack and made sure as he stands up that he will not get back up to attack. Scott walks over to Sivanna and heals her back.

"Did I do something wrong to anger him?"

They both look over at Jack who is still lying in the grass with his chest slowly going up and down.

"No. It is something he has been fighting with all his life, even before I met him. When he just gets a little upset he just freaks."

Sivanna walks over to Jack who is still lying in the grass. She stands above as his eyes pop open. He looks up at Sivanna who puts her hand out to him. He takes hold of it and Sivanna pulls him to his feet. Jack looks away in disgust at himself, their hands still holding each other.

"Jack, I am alright. I now know that I must be careful from now on with you."

"But, I could have really hurt you."

He lets go of Sivanna's hand and turns away. Sivanna places her hand on his arm.

"But you are still a good fighter Jack."

Jack still kept his back towards Sivanna.

"Scott do you mind going back and getting some water for us."

"Sure."

Scott heads back to the village and Jack watches as he disappears into the trees out of the corner of his eye. Sivanna reaches out to Jack.

"Jack…."

Jack turns and hugs Sivanna and buries his face into her shoulder.

"I couldn't control. My eyes saw a dark tunnel and you at the other end. I became so angry. I…..I couldn't stop it. I couldn't stop it."

Sivanna surprised by the hug, gently hugs back.

"Everything is alright now Jack. I will help you in any way to help you control this."

Jack looks up to Sivanna and smiles. Then they both head back to the village, got a drink, and Suki, Scott, and Jack head off to bed. As Scott walks back to his hut with Jack he hugs Jack by his shoulders and both laugh as the continued on their way. Once they were out of sight only Sivanna and Xolstice sit in front the fire.

"I hope the boys will be ready enough for what is coming."

Xolstice turns to Sivanna.

"The Blood Moon is only five moons away. I fear that we will not be ready. They never fought something like this before."

"Sivanna, don't get yourself in a twist. Even when everything seems dark there is always light to balance it out. Darkness will never have total control."

"I know but Nightmare is different. If he ends the bloodline to the moon goddess, he will have the power to end anything and everything and no light will prevail."

Xolstice pats Sivanna's hand.

"If he gets the chance. If you keep thinking this way you won't let light have a fighting chance."

Then Xolstice gets up and walks away into the night leaving Sivanna alone by the dimming fire. She pulls her robe closer to her neck feeling the cool breeze blowing by. She sighs and looks up at the bright white moon shining down on the trees below. She closes her eyes. *Please Moon Goddess, Luma Guah, I pray to you please don't let Nightmare take from me what I care for most, please, not again.*

Chapter 11

Once again, back in the foyer. Katz is carefully detailing all the woodwork of the railings with wax. She would cover them in a cloudy haze and buff them out until they are shiny and new. As she continues farther and farther up the staircase she came closer and closer to the broken window atop the stairs. She stops what she is doing and walks slowly up the stairs. When she gets to the top she stops right in front of the window. From top to bottom in its very center all the beautiful stained glass is gone. Katz steps closer to the window and small cracking sound came from above her and she looks up. She quickly dodges as the glass shatters at her feet. She watches as the glass glitters as its spreads across the floor. Katz walks over the broken glass and stands behind the railing looking out to the court yard. Across the way all that is seen are just shades of gray. All but ash covers the ground where bright green grass and beautiful flowers grew. Huge bushes of brightly colored berries and flowers. The sweet smell of flowers used to fill the air with a wonderful aroma. In the center of the garden lies the fountain. A simple, yet beautiful three tiered fountain. Water shoots from its spout at the top and falls down to the second, then third, and finally to its base to create a pool of water around the tiers. Around its base on the outside used to be a ring of beautiful white roses. In the moonlight they seem to emanate a pale bluish-purple glow. What a beauty they were, but now nothing is left but ash and a quiet fountain no longer flowing with water. Katz began to turn away until she sees something catch her eye. She notices something shining from the garden. Katz heads down to the kitchen door where Vladmir brought her in from the fire. She opens the door and an ashy wind blows past her. She walks across the barren ground towards the fountain and kneels down to the ground. She pushes some ash away to find a little blue seed. Next to the seed a flat stone protrudes from the ground underneath the ash. Katz brushes the ash off gently from the stone. An inscription starts to appear on the stone. Written in beautiful, cursive writing it says *Time flies. Suns rise and shadows fall. Let time go by. Love is forever over all.* Katz sighs as she reads the inscription. Those words are filled with so much love. So, Katz carefully picks up the seed and heads into the kitchen. She grabs a towel from her supplies, wraps it up, and places it into her pocket. Then she took another towel and takes some ash on her finger and writes a note. She goes back to the foyer to continue her work polishing the wood work.

Hours pass by as Katz waits for Vladmir to appear. She works from room to room, cleaning, waiting for Vladmir. Before Katz is taken back to her room she places the seed and note behind the banister on the left side of the staircase. She looks about the room saddened by the absence of Vladmir. Hat plops into the foyer and leads Katz away to her room. The foyer sits in silence as the dust falls shining in the moonlight that came through two windows. It falls like gentle snow silently to the ground. Vladmir appears near the main foyer window looking out to his lifeless garden. He sighs as he closes his eyes thinking of the past as it once was before all of this happened. A breeze blows by him causing him to look down the stairwell. A little white blip pokes in and out between the bars of the railing. He walks down the stairs and kneels down on the last step and reaches in between and pulls out a piece of white cloth. As he lifts the cloth to his face to examine it a second piece falls out to the floor. He picks up the cloth and folds it open and sees a note written on it.

Even though times may seem bleak, there is always hope to shine in the darkness.

Vladmir went to unfold the other piece of cloth when laughter interrupted him. He walks towards the study room door and quietly listens from outside the door.

Nightmare stares outside the window into the starless sky and glares at the moon.

"I will be rid of you one day. On the night of the Blood Moon you will be gone."

Vladmir moves closer to the door.

Hat smiles evilly.

"Yesss Massster. You will soon be massster of the dark. Massster of all. Heh Heh Heh."

"Yes. Once I destroy the bloodline to the Moon Goddess nothing will stop me. Once she is dead."

Nightmare looks back out the window with his red glaring red eyes.

"I will rule this world and the next as supreme."

Nightmare and Hat manically laugh into the night and their laughter rings into the foyer where Vladmir crouches silently in front of the door to the study. Vladmir looks down at his hand and opens the cloth. Deep inside the folds of the cloth lays a single pale blue seed. He stands up holding the cloth and the seed in his hand and heads for the dark corner of the room and vanishes, appearing back in his room. He reaches for his cape that hung on an old coat rack and stands in front of the mirror. He fastens the cape around his neck and straightens it out. It is long, black, and feels like silk. The underside of the cape is a deep crimson red. He looks up at himself in the mirror and stares back into his eyes. Then he looks down at the seed that he holds in his hand and places it in his pocket. He knows what he has to do now. Now it is the time to escape the castle. He won't let Nightmare ruin the life of anyone else.

She sits in the middle of the floor in the light of the moon. The shadows of the bars cascade over her, reminding her of her imprisonment. As she holds her knees close to her she fuddles with her necklace in between her fingers, feeling the cold stone. Katz closes her eyes thinking back to her friends and grandmother. The fun times they used to have. They used to run around and play pranks on one another and just had fun. She also misses her grandmother's cooking. Every day she has been here, rations have been very meager. She sighs and stares off into a sad abyss, into the endless darkness. Then Katz feels a presence behind her. She looks back to see Vladmir standing in far corner of the room. As she began to face away Vladmir appears in front of her. Both of their eyes lock on to one another waiting for what will happen next. Vladmir reaches out with his hand towards Katz. She looks back confused but curious. Vladmir continues to stand there.

"Do you trust me?"

"What do you mean?"

"I need to get you out of the castle."

Katz begins to feel worried.

"Why?"

"I can't discuss this right now. You just have to trust me."

Katz hesitates before reaching for Vladmir's hand. He pulls her up and off the floor and looks into her eyes.

"You must remain silent until I say it is safe to talk."

Katz nods her head and Vladmir takes her by the hand. He leads her to the dark corner of the room. For a moment Katz believes that they are going to run into the wall and then in a blink of an eye she is now in the foyer. She looks behind her to see grayish-black smoke dissipate into the air and reveal a dark corner of the room. Vladmir leads them to the side of the stairwell. He grabs the knob at the end of the railing and twists twice counter clockwise. A soft scraping sound is heard from the left side of the stairwell. They walk over to see a secret opening within the staircase and enter the passage as the door closes quietly behind them. Vladmir takes a torch and lights it with an already lit torch that is hanging on the wall. They walk forward down a flight of stone stairs. Cold condensation drips from the ceiling and dark greenish-black moss grows in the cracks of the stone that make up the walls of the passage. Once they reach the end of the passage, Vladmir hands the torch to Katz. He feels the wall and pulls out a loose brick from the wall. He reaches in and pushes on something. Clinks and clanks, as if a machine, wind and turn in the wall. Then with a solid THUMP and door slides open. Vladmir takes the torch and places it in the holder on the outside and the door closes, with stone against stone, grinding against each other. The passage ends in an old armory. Suits of armor line up on either side of the hallway locked in permanent battle, some with axes and others with long swords. Vladmir walks down to the end of the hallway to a knight that stands strong and straight facing them. In its tarnished metal hands is a sword or what is left of it, just the handle. It looks like the letter "T" with two sphere shapes on its left and right sides. There is nothing special looking about. Vladmir reaches out and pries the sword out of the knight's cold metal hands. Then they turn around and take the passage back up to the foyer. Once again they disappear in a dark corner and appearing in another. Katz is now somewhere she has never seen before in the castle. Vladmir walks over to take items out of the cupboard and place it into the bag. As he went around Katz looks about the room. A simple bed lies in the far corner of the room, an old couch, a fireplace, whose warmth you can still feel even though the fire is long gone, and a beautiful red chair that sits before the fireplace. Katz went up to the chair and feels the soft cloth of the chair and twirls its tassels. She walks over to the fireplace and tries to warm herself by the dying coals. She looks up on the fireplace's mantle and notices a vase. She couldn't believe her eyes! A single rose from the garden still glows in the night. It floats there motionless, weightless in its vase. Katz went to go touch the rose when Vladmir's hand came by and plucks it right out of the vase. He holds the rose close to his face smelling its fragrance. He closes his eyes remembering *her.* He twirls the rose, thinking. Katz just watches waiting to see what he is going to do with the rose. Vladmir opens his eyes, kisses the rose, and places it back into it vase once more. Katz gazes upon the rose.

"Katz."

Katz looks over to Vladmir who is standing next to an open closet. He feels on the inside on the doorway and pulls down on a lever. Stone grinds as another secret passage reveals itself. Vladmir lights another torch and walks into the passage. Katz hesitates then follows him. The closet door closes by itself allowing the passage's door to close. This passage is different from the last. Its walls are made of cold dirt and roots of trees weave in and out of the ceiling. The air is cold, damp, and the sound of water dripping echoes in the tunnel. Katz starts to feel a little anxious.

"Vladmir?"

"Shhhh, yes?"

"Why is there.."

She steps in a puddle and quickly jumps away and squeezes Vladmir's hand.

"..So much water?"

Vladmir looks back to see Katz is becoming very nervous. Her ears lay back on her head and she fuddles with her necklace. She is looking every which way as if looking out for something.

"There is no need to worry this tunnel hasn't collapsed in many years."

"IT COLLAPSED?! FROM WATER?!"

Katz pulls her hand from Vladmir's and freezes in fear. Vladmir turns around with the light of the torch lighting their faces. He could see absolute fear in her eyes.

"We must continue down this tunnel before a rainstorm comes by. This tunnel may fill with water."

He takes Katz's hand and she runs past him. She pulls him, quickening the pace, running for the end of the tunnel. The fire flickers in the wind blowing passed. They reach the end of the tunnel to an old wooden door and Katz frantically searches for a way to open the door.

"OHHHH! HOW DO YOU OPEN THIS DOOR!?"

Katz feels the wall up and down looking for a secret switch of some sort. She couldn't find one. Her heart begins to beat rapidly. She can't get out. Vladmir walks by her and pushes on the door. The door opens to a ladder going up a stone-walled tunnel. She rushes passed Vladmir and charges up the ladder. Vladmir closes the door, puts out the torch, and follows Katz up the ladder. Katz climbs over the edge of the hole and falls on the ground. She slams her back up against the stone wall and breathes in heavily trying to calm down. Vladmir comes up and swings one leg over the wall and lands on his feet. He dusts himself off and reaches a hand out to Katz.

"See, I told you it wouldn't collapse."

Katz takes in a deep breath and takes hold of Vladmir's hand and he pulls her to her feet.

A familiar plopping noise echoes down the hallway. It approaches the door to the boiler room. It pushes open the door. Hat snickers and calls out.

"Hey kitty, kitty, where are you?"

When the door fully opens to Hat's horror Katz is not in her room. No one is in there. It slams the door closed and grumbles to itself. It plops down to Vladmir's room expecting to see the two love birds to be chatting to one another. It knocks on the door.

"Heysss, you two love birdsss."

Once again no one is in the room. It looks everywhere in the room and could not find them anywhere. It starts to get frantic and starts searching the whole castle. It looks in the kitchen, what is left of the garden, the library, the foyer, the bathroom, everywhere. Katz and Vladmir are nowhere to be found. Cold stricken horror fills Hat's mind. It has to go tell Nightmare that Vladmir and Katz have escaped. Hat slowly plops back to the study where Nightmare waits for its report. Hat shivers in fear as it slowly pushes the door open leaving just a crack big enough for Nightmare to see it. Hat clears its throat.

"Nightmare."

"Yes?"

"Um…uh….hmm…ehem…ah…"

Nightmare glares at Hat.

"WHAT!?"

"Katz and Vladmir have esssscaped, massster."

Hat cringes in fear of what might come next. A cold chill enveloped it. It opens it eyes to see Nightmare looking back out the window. A deep laughter comes from Nightmare and Hat looks back all confused.

"I know they have escaped. I allowed them to."

Hat stares back in shock.

"But, but, youss need hersss for the Blood Moonsss?! For the ritualsss!"

A crooked smile slowly appears across Nightmare's face in the reflection of the window.

"I know but these two will lead me to *them.* Vladmir is going to lead me to where the White Witches are hiding. In turn using him to destroy them and ending the bloodline to the moon goddess."

Nightmare laughs into the night as he watches his diabolical plan in his head play out in his favor right before him. Hat chuckles.

"Ah, thatss good. Such foolssss."

Nightmare continues to watch out the window, his plan unfolding before him.

Katz looks back to see that they have came out of an old well on the right side of the castle. Her heart leaps for joy. She is finally out of the castle. She looks about her and just sees the night sky, full of stars, and the moon shining brightly. Surrounding the castle is a dark dense forest. As you look into the trees, in between the trunks and branches it gets darker and darker the farther you go in. It is the kind of darkness where you feel that someone or something is watching you. Vladmir takes Katz to the back of the castle where there is a large opening of grass and at its very edge is the forest. Vladmir and Katz ran towards the forest. When they reach the edge, the trees are bent into an arch shape as if showing the entrance to the forest. Vladmir pulls out the hilt of the broken sword and hands it to Katz.

"What do I do with this?"

Vladmir stands staring up at the top of the arched trees.

"You place the gem of your necklace into the sword's hilt."

Katz looks down to see a space open for a small stone of some type. She looks at her necklace and back at the hilt. They were the same size. She takes off her necklace and pulls the gem off the chain and then places the chain back around her neck. Then she places the gem into the hilt where the handle meets the two pieces that stick out at either side.

"So just like this?"

The sword began to quiver in her hand. The sword hilt began to change. It began to fill with a glowing silver shine where ever metal looked dull and gray, and where the gem is placed on either side a shape forms. It takes the shape of a crescent moon with its tips pointing to the sky. Three pale blue streaks of light shoot from the sword's hilt and fly to the sky with tails of light following behind them. The streaks of light came back down and where an empty space was now there are three glowing pale blue blades that hover just above the hilt. The sword stops quivering and lies quiet in Katz's hands. Katz looks in amaze and shock.

"How did you know the sword was going to do that?"

Vladmir looks at the sword.

"I didn't. I read a legend in a book about the knight that used to wield that very sword. The only thing it said was "The One who holds the Stone of Pure will bring life back to the sword once more.""

Katz looks back at the blade she now holds, feeling the cold shining silver hilt in her hands.

"Now you need to swing the sword in a straight down attack."

Katz gives Vladmir a confusing look.

"What? Why?"

"To break the barrier that surrounds the castle. Nightmare said at the forest's edge lays a barrier that only a strong force may break. So, swing the sword."

Katz takes the sword and lifts it above her head.

"Like this?"

Then she strikes down in front of her. A wave of purple lightning spreads out to the top of the arch and out. Its light shoots across the forest edge breaking the barrier. Then a gentle breeze crawls out of the forest and past Vladmir and Katz. Then a high pitched shriek screams into the night. A dense black fog forms behind them making the castle disappear from their sights. The ground begins to quake as if something is coming up and through the dirt. Katz screams as a sharp-clawed hand reaches up and out of the ground in front of her. As far as they can see in the fog there were more. In a distance one has fully emerge from ground. It is nothing like Katz or Vladmir has seen before. It is a ghost-like figure covered in stitched rags but black palms and claw-like fingers takes place of hands. Its head, also made of stitched patches, comes back to a point but the faces are even stranger. Their eyes are buttons. One is a dusty blue and the other a dull purple. They are stitched on by an X-shaped stitch interwoven between four holes. Yet what scares Katz the most is the crooked, sinister smile across their faces. Katz falls back into Vladmir and drops the sword and it goes back to its original form. Katz reaches down for the gem and Vladmir grabs the hilt. As far as their eyes could see in the dense fog, there must have been a hundred of these things standing before them. Then one in the very middle rises above the rest. It stares down at Vladmir and Katz. A moment of silence stands between them. Then it screeches into the air with a horrifying scream that brings chills to your bones. The rest join in filling the air with their horrible screams and then went after Vladmir and Katz. Vladmir grabs Katz by the hand and pulls her into the forest. They rush pass tree after tree trying to escape these creatures. In the dark forest nothing is seen, the only thing they could hear is the shrieks and shrills behind them, getting closer. Katz brings her gem to her face and begins to pray. Vladmir continues to pull Katz through the trees trying to avoid any slip-ups. Then a blue glow emanates from Katz's hand. Vladmir stops and looks back. Katz opens her hand allowing the glow to get brighter. The glow lights up their faces revealing Katz's face wet with tears. Vladmir watches behind her with a stern look, ready to fight with what may come through the darkness, but nothing did. They could see the creatures' faces popping in and out the darkness but coming no closer. The screams became quiet and the dark fog began to back away, back to the castle. Then all became quiet. The light of the moon peeked in and out of the branches that hang above them. Vladmir scans the area around him making sure nothing is watching them. He continues into the forest and looks behind to see Katz is not following him. He approaches her and she hugs him burying her face into his chest. She brings to cry. Vladmir, who is quite surprised, gently places his arms around her.

"It will be alright. No one is going to harm you."

Katz looks up at him with pleading eyes as tears roll down her cheeks. He wraps one arm around her and holds her hand with another and they both continue to walk into the forest not knowing what may be around the next corner.

Chapter 12

They reach a small clearing where the moon shines the brightest. They sit against a tree to rest. Vladmir rests his back on the tree and Katz rests against his chest. She falls asleep, tired from her ordeal. Vladmir looks up to the moon and sighs. He looks down to see Katz finally calm and peaceful. He brushes his fingers through her hair and letting it gently fall onto her face. He sighs and feeling something he hasn't felt for awhile. He feels peaceful and what a wonderful feeling that is. He smiles down at Katz as she sleeps then he heard something. Katz awakes looking around with sleepy eyes.

"What? Did you hear something?"

Vladmir gets up and looks about. Katz sits up against the tree and yawns. Rustling of tree branches breaks the silence. A quiet lip-smacking sound bounces across the canopy. Katz stands up and dusts herself off.

"What is ….."

"Shhh."

Vladmir watches the trees above watching where the leaves are falling. Katz follows his gaze. Vladmir picks up a rock and then chucks it into the trees. A soft THUNK and a loud THUD are heard as a bush rattles nearby. Vladmir and Katz walk over to the site the sound came from. On the ground sits a rabbit rubbing his right eye. He looks up to see Vladmir and Katz looking down. He grunts.

"Why?! Why is it always the eye?"

The rabbit gets up and picks up his fork and spoon. He looks up at Katz and Vladmir. With a crazed look, he twitches, and a piece of his ear looks like a piece has been bitten out of it. The rabbit stands in a defensive stance, his eyes slowly going back and forth between the two invaders. Vladmir picks up another rock and tosses it into the air and catches it.

"I will get you. One day!"

The rabbit hops back into the trees and disappears from site. Vladmir drops the rock and walks back to the clearing and picks up his bag. Katz comes up from behind him.

"Who was that?"

Vladmir just smiles.

"He calls himself "The Cannibal Rabbit". I ran into him one day when I was outside the castle. I was near the entrance when he jumped out at me. I took hold of him and tried to shove him back into the hole in the ground that he came out of. He freaked out and, ha, I love this part. He looked up at me and said "I do not like being in TIGHT TINY HOLES! I am claustrophobic! I prefer to live in the trees, plus I am going to eat you!""

Katz looks at him confused.

"I'm serious. I guess he thought I was an over sized rabbit. Ha Ha Ha. He eventually left and I didn't see him until now."

Katz looks at Vladmir and pulls on his ears.

"Hmmm, just a little."

Then they both laugh. They pack up everything and continue to head farther and deeper into the forest.

Katz and Vladmir come to a wide open clearing as they crest the hill. Down below lay a beautiful lake where the stars reflect their beauty in the water. It stretches across the land in the shape of the moon. It has been many hours since they had a nice, long rest. So Vladmir takes blankets out of the bag and gives one to Katz. He gets wood from the forest floor and lights a fire to keep them warm. They both sleep on separate sides of the fire. Vladmir faces the sky and closes his eyes and Katz turns to Vladmir. Katz wraps up tightly and closes her eyes.

"Good night Vladmir."

He looks over at her and back to the sky.

"Good night Katz."

Then they both fall into a deep sleep around a warm fire.

Images coming into site are blurry and unfocused. The sounds are muffled and wordless. Then an image comes clear, its voice becoming less foggy. A woman is seen sitting on the ground wounded and pale. Her face Vladmir cannot see. She whimpers and cries and her face looks up to Vladmir.

"Vladmir? Why? Why didn't save me? I thought you loved me?"

She buries her face into her hands and cries uncontrollably. Vladmir reaches out to touch her. Then Nightmare's face takes hers and he charges at Vladmir. Nightmare slithers into Vladmir's body. He falls to his knees and crawls to a nearby puddle. When he looks into it he can only see Nightmare's face, laughing.

"YOUR SOUL IS MINE!
MWHAHAHAHAHAHAHAHA!"

Vladmir wakes with a start and is panting heavily.
Sweat beads down his cold, clammy face. He rubs his
hand over his face and covers his mouth and closes his
eyes. He flings the blanket off and blows out the last of
the burning embers. Vladmir notices Katz shivering
underneath her blanket, unclips his cape, and places it
over Katz. Vladmir heads down a deep slope and comes
to the shore of the lake. He kneels down and takes off
his vest and unbuttons his shirt so it does not get wet.
Then he splashes his face with the cold water trying to
rid himself of his dream.

Katz yawns and rubs her eyes. As she
gets up she notices Vladmir is gone and his cape lies
across her legs. She stands and wraps the blanket
around her shoulders, picks up Vladmir's cape, and
stands at the top of the slope going down to the lake.
She didn't realize it at first but the lake is in the shape of
a crescent moon. The water is calm and the moon and
stars shine in its reflection. Tall grasses pop up here and
there around the lake's edge. Then surrounding the
whole lake is the never-ending forest. It seems that in
every which way you look there are always trees. Katz
notices something moving in front of the lake's edge.
She walks down the steep slope and comes up to the

lake's edge. She sees Vladmir on his knees washing his face. Katz walks up and kneels next to him. He splashes his face once more, closes his eyes, and takes in a deep breath. Katz looks at him and notices a scar going across his chest from his left shoulder down to his right side.

"Vladmir are you OK?"

Vladmir looks over to see that Katz is looking at his scar. He quickly buttons up his shirt and places on his vest. He looks down as he buttons his vest.

"Yeah, I'm fine."

"What about....."

"It's an old scar, it is in the past."

Vladmir gets up and dusts off his pants and he keeps his back towards Katz. Katz could sense a feeling of uneasiness and avoidance from Vladmir about the subject. She sits on her heels and looks about for something to change the subject. Then she remembers that she has his cape. She gets it and dusts it off too.

"Here, thought you might want this back."

When she looks up, she notices Vladmir is not in front of her. She feels a cold breeze behind her and looks. Vladmir pops out of a black-grayish cloud carrying his bag and some kindling for a fire. He sat his bag near a big, old, tree and places the kindling not too far from the tree. Vladmir takes out two stones from his bag and starts a new warm burning fire. Katz walks over and warms her hands by the fire. Vladmir motions to her to sit down and he sits down as well. He reaches into his bag and pulls out some bread and some dried meat. He hands some to Katz, takes some for himself, and places the rest away. They eat quietly listening to the wind blow through the leaves of the trees and the crackling of the fire. Katz's food becomes a lump in her throat as she grows with anticipation for something to break the silence between them. Vladmir looks up to see Katz fidgeting while looking back and forth between him and her food. Vladmir reaches into his bag and pulls out the hilt of the sword.

"I can see that you are not good with swords, yes?"

Katz looks away in embarrassment.

"Well, while we are out here I am going to train you."

Katz looks at him curiosity filling her eyes.

"Train me for what?"

"To be able to face Nightmare. He will be looking for you to fulfill his plan. You need to be able to fight."

"What is he planning with me? What did I do to him?"

"I am not sure what his plan is but you must be able to defend yourself. The one thing he will use against you is your fears."

Katz's face grows cold. Then she looks out to the lake, Vladmir smiles.

"I do recall that you told me you do not like water. That is something he will use against you. Well, I am going help you face that fear by showing you how to swim."

Katz looks at him like he is crazy. She quickly looks at the lake and back at Vladmir and shakes her head.

"No. I will not get in the water."

Vladmir stands with his hands held behind him.

"If you do not learn then Nightmare has already beaten you."

Katz turns away on her knees, sits, looks away pouting, and crosses her arms in a defiant manner. Vladmir just shakes his head.

"I promise we will start small."

Katz looks over her shoulder with a serious look on her face.

"You promise?"

Vladmir places one of his hands over his heart.

"Promise."

Katz takes off her socks and shoes as slowly as possible so she doesn't have to go in the water so quickly. Vladmir takes off his socks, shoes, and his vest. He folds his vest neatly and lays it on top of his shoes. He takes off his gloves and sits them on top of his vest. Vladmir walks over to the water's edge and steps in so the water just covers his toes. Katz slowly gets up and slowly walks to the water. She digs her toes into the ground while her heart pounds in her chest. Vladmir reaches a hand out to her and waits. A moment of silence hangs between them as Katz nervously watches the water lap up and down the bank. Vladmir stands and waits.

"Please take your time."

Katz cautiously grabs his hand and Vladmir turns to go into deeper water. As soon as her toes touch the water she jumps on Vladmir's back. Her arms and legs wrapped around him, tightly. Katz starts to climb up Vladmir trying to get farther away from the water. Now she is nearly on the top of his head and Vladmir is doing his best to keep calm and keep balance.

"You know we are in ankle deep water."

Katz looks down at the water. Underneath all the water lies a monotone pattern of pebbles and rocks that spread across the sandy floor. The image of the pebbles ripples every time they move. Katz goes to look over her shoulder and causes Vladmir to go off balance and both Vladmir and Katz fall into the water, and Katz is first to hit the water. Vladmir feels Katz let go and surfaces. He looks to see Katz is already out of the water, dripping wet. Her ears lay flat against her head as she rubs her arms to warm herself. Vladmir walks up to her and motions her back into the water. Katz doesn't move.

"You need to get back in the water in order to learn to swim."

Katz sputters out quiet words.

"No. I can't."

Katz looks away and shivers.

"We will keep to the shallows and no further. I will be right beside you."

Katz looks at the water and slowly inches her way in. As soon as the water touches her she backs out of the water and looks away.

"Why are you so afraid of water?"

Katz continues to look away.

"I know it is silly to be afraid of water but I just am. I'm afraid of falling in and not coming back up."

"Katz."

She looks up at Vladmir with worried eyes.

"I won't let you fall."

She smiles a weak smile and tries getting back into the water. Now she is in the water with it up to her ankles. Katz moves her feet in the water letting it fall around her toes. She feels a little relaxed and gets spooked when she hears the water slosh around her as she continues deeper into the water. Now the water is just above her waist and she is standing next to Vladmir. Then Vladmir began instructing Katz in how to swim from the basic doggy paddle to a back stroke. She didn't stay long but long enough to get the basic idea of swimming. Now they are both back up on the shore. Katz is completely wrapped head to toe in a blanket in front of the fire. The fire crackles and pops in front of her as she watches the flames try to reach for the sky. She inches closer to get warmer faster. Vladmir leans up against the old tree and pulls the blanket up to his shoulders.

"Well, that is enough for one day. Good night."

He closes his eyes and relaxes. Katz watches as Vladmir falls into a deep sleep. A rustle of leaves in the forest interrupts her thoughts and she looks out to the forest. The noise has ceased but the feeling of being watched creeps into her mind. She gets up and leans up against the tree next to Vladmir. Katz curls up and tries to make herself comfortable on the hard ground and she too falls fast asleep.

Katz's eyes flutter open to another sunless day. The stars and the moon greet her once more. She stretches and lets out a big yawn. Then she realizes there is a sound in the air. It is music. It is very beautiful as it flows through the air. The sweet song serenades the air and makes Katz feel light and carefree. Then the music turns sad, reminiscent of a song for a lost one. Katz gets up and wanders around the lake trying to find the source of the music. She turns a corner to a small green patch in front of the lake that is surrounded by trees, and standing at its edge is Vladmir. His eyes are closed as he plays his violin. Katz has never seen a more beautiful violin. Its deep blue color shines in the moon's light revealing the faint white roses that decorate its body. The neck of the violin is a deeper blue with a blue rose at the end. The strings sing their music as Vladmir glides his bow across them. Vladmir hasn't notice Katz standing there so Katz sits down in the grass and just listens. Vladmir sways with the flow of his music. His bow shoots up sharply and vibrates to fade the music out. Vladmir sighs and places his bow and violin to his one side and opens his eyes. To his surprise he sees Katz looking up at him from the grass. He kneels down and places the violin into the case.

"Sorry if I woke you."

"You didn't. Actually, it was quite nice to wake up to it. It was very beautiful."

Vladmir picks up his case and walks back to the old tree to place it back into his bag.

"Well, thank you."

Katz gets up and follows him to the tree. Vladmir walks out of the forest with two long, thick branches. He throws one to Katz and she catches it.

"Hit me."

Katz looks at him in confusion.

"Why?"

Vladmir stands to his side one hand on his hip and the other holding the branch.

"Attack me."

"Why would I hit you?"

"We are starting your training. Now, hit me."

Katz looks away twisting her hand around the branch.

"I have no reason to. I wouldn't hit you Vladmir. I can't."

Vladmir turns, in frustration, into the forest and comes back out with a large leaf. He dips it into the water and pulls it two ends together to hold the water in. He walks over to Katz who watches the leaf as he comes near. He leans out towards her.

"Hit me."

Katz backs off with the branch held out in front of her. Vladmir rolls his eyes and turns away. Then he quickly turns back around and lets go of one of the ends of the leaf sending the water flying. It lands all over Katz making her soaking wet. Katz looks back at Vladmir with disgust and he just smiles.

"Hit me, you have a reason now."

Katz lunges out and strikes straight down at Vladmir. He moves off to the side as the branch lands right in front of him.

"Good, now again."

Katz lifts her branch and runs up to Vladmir and swings to his left side. Vladmir stops it with one swift move. He smiles and Katz glares back. She brings the branch back and swings from the right and he blocks it. Every attack she gives is blocked by Vladmir. She backs off to catch her breath. She wipes her brow and watches Vladmir. He comes straight at her and swings at her head. She ducks and swings for his feet. He jumps and lands on her branch and she pulls it out from underneath him. Vladmir flips backwards and lands on his feet waiting for the next attack. She swings and Vladmir grabs her branch pulls her forward then pushes her back with his branch to the ground, the end of the branch just above her throat. They both stay in position for a moment and Vladmir pulls the branch away. He pulls her off the ground and she dusts off.

"You have the fight in you it just needs more improvement. You left too many open spaces where I could have taken you down easily. Even if you are angered you must think your strategy before attacking."

For the rest of the day Vladmir teaches Katz the basics of fighting from initiating an attack to defending herself from one. This time Vladmir didn't hold back and attacks her at every open space she gives him. She eventually learns to not to leave herself so open to attack. She sits down after awhile and takes a drink of water from a canister Vladmir gives her. Katz's body is sore and feels like it is covered in bruises. Vladmir rubs his upper arm.

"Not bad. You did get me good there. Just remember not to hesitate after hitting your target because they won't."

Katz is so worn out she just nods her head. Then something catches her eye. She looks out over the lake to see something glowing in the distance. She stands up to get a better look. The creature is translucent and just floating above the water. It had a pale yellow glow. Katz walks down the edge of the lake to try to get closer. When she gets close enough she finally sees what it is. To her amazement the creature looks like a jellyfish, swimming in the air. Its body ripples with each movement and two fragile fins flap on either side. Its tentacles gently glide through the air. Katz reaches out to touch it and then more of them reveal themselves around her and across the lake. She looks across the lake to see different pale shades of yellow, pink, and purple. Katz watches in awe as they float about the lake. Vladmir comes up next to her.

"I do recall from a book I have read that these creatures are called Glighten. They are only seen at night over bodies of water."

They continue to watch the Glightens until they fade back into the darkness from which they came. Vladmir went and got some more wood for the fire and Katz stays behind poking the burning embers with a stick. He places the wood on top of the hot embers and some dry grass to get the wood to catch. Once again they get wrapped into their blankets to get ready for another night's rest. Vladmir lies on his back looking up at the starry sky. Tomorrow they must continue their journey into the forest and meet the Gate Keeper at the Entrance to Azmala, who guards the entrance to either world. Tomorrow they must face Archer the Guardian of the Gate.

Chapter 13

Once again in the dark, quiet forest Vladmir and Katz walk through the tightly woven trees. Many of the trees' roots rise above the ground twisting into one another. The wind gently blows at the leaves and branches. The moon pops in and out of the canopy. Then the air suddenly becomes cold as if snow is lying on the ground. Katz rubs her arms to keep warm and then Vladmir stops her. They both look up to see trees intertwined into one another forming a tall archway. Vladmir and Katz continue through the archway to an open area. Everything around them had no color. The ground, the leaves, the sky are all shades of gray. In front of them lies a great door with a black-barred fence on either side of it. The door is a bright-glowing white with sparkling silver detailing. As they walk closer to the door a dark mass begins to form in front of the door. Then a floating being lies before them. Its head had a hood with two large horns sticking out of the top. In the hood, where a head should be, lies a dark-stone like mask with white sideways diamond-shaped eyes and on the right eye a red "S" shaped mark with slashes right across it. The mask's mouth is only five vertical slits. It wears a dark green scarf around its neck. Over its dark green long sleeved shirt is a brown leather vest. Two buckles come across the chest and one around the hips holding a small dagger. A single dark leather strap sits diagonally across its chest and it holds a bow and arrows. The bow itself is unique. Where the tip of the arrow lies when pulled back is a dragon's head with its mouth wide open revealing sharp teeth. Upon the being's shoulders is armor plating with spikes poking out of it. On its leather gloves are two iron plates lying against the back of its hands and where there are supposed to be feet are none. Vladmir and Katz stand before the being, which speaks out in a deep, loud voice.

"Who dare stand be forth the Gate to Azmala? For I am the Guardian, Archer."

"It is I, Vladmir, and my friend. We wish to gain access to Azmala."

Archer places a hand before them.

"No."

"Why?"

"I have been summoned by a greater force then I to stop you and not allow admittance to Azmala's Gate."

"We must gain entrance to Azmala! It is of great importance!"

"You will not pass."

Vladmir pulls out his dagger from his belt and holds it in front of his face which is glaring at Archer.

"Fine, no matter what you say we will go through that door!"

Archer pulls the bow from his back and reaches for an arrow.

"Then your fate has been decided."

Archer pulls back on the arrow and shoots it towards Vladmir and Katz. Vladmir pulls Katz out of the way as the arrow digs into the ground beside them. They race to the trees as arrows follow behind them. As they dive into the bushes Archer stands guard in front of the door, bow at the ready.

"Come out and face your fate."

Archer waits for a reply and when none is heard, he shoots an arrow into the bushes. Vladmir flinches as the arrow grazes his left arm. He grabs his arm and Katz looks over with concern. Vladmir puts his finger to his mouth.

"Shhh, I'm alright."

Vladmir looks towards the bush as if he could see through it and watches Archer. He stands up to see Archer is not there. He scans the open area to see where Archer may appear. Katz screams and Vladmir turns to see what happened. Archer grabs and takes Katz in front of the door. Katz fights his grip with no luck, Vladmir jumps out of the bushes and stands before Archer. Archer takes out an old, simple hourglass. It shakes the hourglass so a sharp tip appears. It takes Katz's arm and pricks it with the point. Her blood seeps into the hourglass changing the white sand to blood red. Katz falls limp in Archer's hand.

"Within an hour of the time now your friend here will cease to live. As the hour grows near she will become weaker, her heart beating slower, until it will be no more."

Vladmir grinds his teeth and glares and grips the dagger in his hand. Anger swells within him and his eyes grow pitch black. A deep menacing growl escapes Vladmir lips. He snarls and disappears into the shadows. Archer looks around to see where Vladmir went. Unknown to Archer, Vladmir reappears in a tree above him and jumps at him dagger just above his head.

"GRRRRAAAAAAAAAAAAAAAAH!"

Vladmir strikes Archer in the back, pulling the dagger down as he falls. Archer drops Katz and falls to the ground. Vladmir removes the dagger and walks in front of Archer. He picks up Katz in his arms and glares down at Archer. Archer looks up to see an evil, dark mass surround Vladmir and his glaring black eyes looking down upon him. Then the mass went away and Vladmir's eyes went back to normal. He picks up the hourglass and runs for the door. The door opens to a white abyss that seems to lead to nowhere. As he passes through the door Archer's voice echoes passed him. *Within the hour your friend will be dead.* Then Vladmir carries Katz into the door and disappears from site, the doors shut, and Archer disappears. The door fades away leaving an open field that continues on into the dark forest. Within the darkness a darker mass appears but not fully formed. A faint laughter echoes from the form and an evil, sharp- toothed smile appears in the blackness.

Through a bright white into a black abyss, time seems to have stopped. Everything is silent except for the air that escapes their lips. They feel weightless and float through the abyss. Then they stop, motionless, and they fall fast in a downward spiral. The doors fly open and Katz and Vladmir fall to the ground, the doors close with a low groan, click, and vanish. Vladmir stands on his feet and picks up Katz once more. With the hourglass in hand he heads for the opening of the forest. He reaches the edge of the forest and stops. Ahead of him a familiar glow lights the trees. Vladmir walks out of the forest and turns his head down so the bright light doesn't blind him. Once his eyes adjusted he turns his head up to the bright light and smiles. He hasn't felt the warmth of the sun's light for a long time. The moon may have given him light but never the warmth that the sun gives. The rays of the sun gently warm his body and he watches as the clouds pass in the light blue sky. He looks down at Katz who he holds closer. Vladmir takes the path ahead of him as fast as he could and hopes it will lead to a town or village that can help them. He runs in and out of trees with the sun pouring its lights through the branches, leaps over roots, and weaves in and out of tall trees. He reaches a wide open clearing upon a hill. Vladmir looks across the field to see a path that is well worn meaning that someone has taken this path more than once. Katz moans and starts to breathe slower. Vladmir races for the path and follows it to a tall old door made of tree trunks. He tries to open the door but it will not open. He rams it with his shoulder to no avail. Vladmir looks up at the door.

"HELLO!? ANYONE THERE!"

There is no answer.

"IS ANYONE THERE?"

The door opens slowly to a young girl. She pokes her head out of the door and sees a man with a young woman in his arms.

"Yes?"

"Please I need your help."

Vladmir holds Katz in her direction. Katz just moans as her only response. The young girl gasps and opens the door further to allow Vladmir and Katz in. The young girl closes the door behind them and leads them into the village. They run down the path and Vladmir is panting hard from running.

"Thank you."

The young girl looks over and smiles.

"Door open for a needy friend."

Vladmir nods his head and continues down the path with the young girl. They come to the open of the village with people who notice them running in. An older lady sees them and runs up to them. Vladmir stops with sweat rolling down his face and completely out of breath. The older lady gasps.

"KATZ?"

She motions for two other people to come help them. They take Katz from Vladmir and before they leave his sight he speaks.

"It...is....a spell....with...."

With a shaking hand he lifts the hourglass with the red sand still pouring into the other chamber. The older lady takes the hourglass and Vladmir collapses from exhaustion. He lies motionless and two other villagers come and place him on a stretcher and carry him away.

Vladmir awakens to a soft touch on his forehead. He opens his eyes to see the young girl placing a wet towel on his head. Then he notices the young girl tying cloth around his upper arm covering his wound. Vladmir lies on a wooden bench with a pillow propping his head up in a wooden hut. He sighs and relaxes for every part of his body ached and felt very tired. He looks over at the young girl who is now holding a cup of water for him to drink. She helps Vladmir sit up and gives him the cup. The cool water feels great and rejuvenates him. He looks out the window and notices the moon is now in the sky. Vladmir tries to get up but the girl stops him.

"I need to check on Katz."

The girl places a hand on his chest allowing him to go no further.

"She's fine, she resting."

"The spell..."

"Spell gone. No more, she better."

Vladmir runs a hand through his hair and relaxes. He sits back and closes his eyes. The young girl hands him another cup of cool water to drink. She gets up and leaves the hut. Vladmir looks about the room. A small basic cot sits in the far corner, and table with a bowl of water and a towel, and a small fire crackling out of a pit. He watches the smoke rise upward and flow through the hole in the ceiling. He hears a small knock and looks towards the door. It is the older lady who he met earlier. She comes over a sits down next to him. She takes his hand into hers and looks at him with tears in her eyes. She smiles.

"Thank you very much for bringing Katz home. Thank you."

The lady gently wraps her arms around Vladmir and hugs him.

"You're welcome."

She dries the tears on her face and reaches her hand out and shakes Vladmir's.

"I am Sivanna. I am Katz's grandmother."

"My name is Vladmir. I am a friend. How is Katz?"

"She is fine. The spell put on her is a minor one and easily dealt with. She is resting in my hut. How are you doing?"

"I am doing fine as well, just tired from earlier. I thank you for your hospitality but I must go now."

Vladmir gets up and Sivanna stops him.

"But you can't."

"I must, I am just happy she is safe now."

"Yes indeed but you are invited to a feast."

"A feast?"

"Yes, in celebration of Katz's coming home and her birthday."

Vladmir looks away knowing that staying here is not safe. He looks back at Sivanna whose eyes are pleading with him to stay. He looks out to the night sky.

"Vladmir?"

He looks in front of him to see Katz standing there, smiling. She looks behind him and she squeals. Katz runs up to her grandmother and gives her the biggest hug. Happy tears came to both of their faces.

"Oh grandma I am so happy to see you again!"

"And so am I to see you my dear."

"I thought I wasn't going to see you again."

Katz and Sivanna continue to chat on while Vladmir stands outside the hut watching the stars shoot by. The bugs chirp and the birds settle in for the night. Vladmir looks up into a tree and spots two birds huddled together to share each other's warmth. Across the field two boys came running to the hut. Vladmir steps out of the way as they charge through the door. They both come in and dog-pile Katz. They all lay on the floor laughing. Katz gets up and hugs the both of them. Scott picks up Katz and spins her in a circle.

"Man Katz, I thought we weren't going to see you again. I felt so bad for leaving you back there."

"Yeah it was driving him nuts more than usual."

Jack laughs as Scott glares at him. Katz just laughs.

"Yeah, I missed the both of you! Being in that castle was the worst thing that ever happened to me."

"We said we were sorry."

Scott and Jack speak in unison. They both look at each other and laugh. Then Scott looks at Katz with big curious eyes.

"So how did you get out of the castle?"

Katz looks about the room and notices Vladmir is not there. She walks over to the doorway and off to her right Vladmir is standing there leaning against the wall staring into the night sky. She looks at him curiously.

"Is everything OK?"

Vladmir looks over with a solemn look.

"Yes."

Katz smiles.

"Good. I want you to meet my friends."

"Your....."

Katz takes Vladmir by the hand and pulls him through the door. Scott, Jack, and Sivanna look at Vladmir and Katz. Vladmir nervously fixes his vest and Katz is bubbling with joy next to him.

"This is who saved me from the castle. Everyone I want you to meet Vladmir."

Vladmir stands up straight.

"Good Evening everyone."

Sivanna smiles, Jack just waves, and Scott just stares back with big eyes of surprise. Katz and Valdmir sit down and both her and her grandmother chat while Vladmir sits quietly. Scott nudges Jack in the side with his elbow.

"What?"

"Do you see what I see?"

"Him."

"What about him?"

Scott looks at Jack with disbelief.

"Don't you see it?"

Jack sits and waits for Scott to continue. Scott moves closer to Jack and whispers.

"He is a vampire."

Jack backs off.

"Are you serious? Scott I told you there is no such thing as vampires."

"But he has the fancy style clothing and all that red and black color."

Jack rolls his eyes.

"That doesn't make him a vampire."

Jack looks up at Katz who moves closer to Vladmir and laughs.

"But there does seem to be something about him that's off."

"Duh, because he is a vampire."

Jack smacks Scott in the back of the head and Scott glares at him as he rubs his head. Sivanna stands up and gets everyone's attention.

"Well we all had a very eventful day and a busy one tomorrow. So lets all head off to bed so we can be ready for tomorrow."

The boys get up and hug Katz and Sivanna good night and head off. Sivanna sends Katz off to her hut and waves. She walks up to Vladmir.

"If you wish to stay, please use this hut here to rest for the night. Good Night Vladmir."

She bows her head and Vladmir bows back. Sivanna heads to her hut and Vladmir heads back into his designated quarters.

Jack wakes up in the middle of the night due to a rustling noise. He looks over to see Scott, who is hiding in his blanket, looking out the window. Jack takes one of his pillows and tosses it at Scott. Scott turns around and tosses the pillow back.

"Shhh, I am on vampire watch."

"Scott, would you just go to bed?"

"Come here Jack."

Jack grunts and sits next to Scott at the window.

"See, look."

Jack looks out the window to see Vladmir standing outside his hut gazing up at the stars, and puffs of white smoke escapes his lips as he breathes into the cold night air.

Jack glares at Scott.

"So, what am I suppose to be looking at."

"Him! He's just standing there."

"So?"

"So?! He is supposed to be asleep like everyone else. Only vampires stay awake at night."

Jack just rolls his eyes in agitation.

"Ever heard of trouble sleeping?"

"He doesn't have trouble sleeping."

Jack grunts and falls back into his bed and closes his eyes. Scott continues to stare out the window.

"I know you're a vampire and I'll prove it."

Scott leans closer to the window making sure that Vladmir won't see him. His eyes continue to watch Vladmir's every move.

Valdmir stares into the night with one question puzzling his mind. *If Nightmare wanted to get to the White Witches so bad, why isn't he here now?*

Chapter 14

Jack wakes up to the morning's warm sun in his face. He looks over at Scott and just chuckles. Scott is plastered to the window fast asleep and is snoring up a storm. Jack walks over to Scott and hits him with a pillow and startles him. Scott looks up at Jack with sleepy eyes.

"What?"

"You feel asleep on the window sill."

Scott rubs and wipes drool quickly off his face. Jack heads out the door and Scott moans and falls back into bed. Then Suki comes running through the door and starts jumping up and down next to Scott's bed.

"SCOTT! Scott, wake up!"

Scott wraps his pillow around his head and moans.

"Scott, time celebrate! Festival Day!"

Scott doesn't move so Suki takes the pillow off of Scott's head. Scott rolls over and sighs.

"You wake?"

"Yes."

Suki claps her hands happily and runs out the door and Scott slowly gets ready for the day. He heads out the door and is stopped by the commotion outside. People are running left and right, hanging up banners and streamers, and gathering flowers to decorate the village. Jack comes up and nudges him with his elbows since his hands were full of things for the festival.

"Come on, you have to help too."

Jack gets pushed along by a very happy Suki. Jack regains his balance and keeps the stuff from falling from his arms.

"Scott, come, help! Such happy day!"

Scott follows Suki and Jack to a really big hut with plumes of smoke rising from the top.

"Scott, help in there, Jack come me."

Jack follows behind Suki and Scott enters the hut and the most delicious smell blows past him. He walks in to see many villagers at work, cutting, cleaning, cooking, and baking a variety of things. Scott looks around the corner to see Sivanna rolling out and weaving dough into braided loaves. She places them onto a flat stone surface and slides it into the hole just above a burning fire. Then she pulls one right out from underneath the fire and aroma of fresh baked bread fills the air. Scott's stomach begins to grumble. Sivanna looks over and passes a slice of fresh, hot bread to Scott.

"Here before you start working."

Sivanna takes Scott to a table in the far back and introduces him to the one of the cooks.

"Scott this is our head cook. You are going to help him prepare the stew for tonight."

Scott and the cook shake hands as Sivanna leaves. The cook leads Scott to an open space on the table and put a basket of vegetables next to him.

"I need you to peel and cut these vegetables into small chunks. Here let me show you."

The cook takes a curved stone utensil with a sharp edge and slowly starts to wind it around the purple potato-like vegetable until all of the skin has fallen off. Then he takes another much larger stone with a leather handle and dices the potato into small cubes. The cook then places the pieces into the pot next to him. Scott nods his head and begins to peel and dice vegetables for the cook.

Jack just stands still as Suki takes things out of his hands to decorate the village with. She hangs up banners, streamers, and lays out blankets around the fire pit for people to sit on later. As Jack stands and waits for his hands to empty he looks around and spots Vladmir. He stands in the shadows cutting wood with a primitive stone ax for the fire pit and for the cooks. Jack looks around for Katz but she is nowhere in sight. He shifts the items in his hands and sees Suki coming back for another banner.

"Hey, Suki, where's Katz?"

"Katz?"

"Yes, where is she?"

"Oh, she get ready for tonight."

"Can I go see her?"

"No. You help me here."

"Well, afterwards?"

"No."

Suki looks at Jack with a stern look and Jack just rolls his eyes. Scott and Sivanna continue to help in the kitchen, Suki and Jack continue to decorate, and Vladmir finally gets to relax from chopping wood. He has been at it since this morning. He takes his cup of water and sits on a log to rest. Katz comes running over and stands next to him. She takes Vladmir by the hand and pulls him to the hut where all the cooking is going on. Jack watches from afar until he could see them no more with an angered look. Katz and Vladmir sneak up to the window near the bakers. Katz first looks into the window and Vladmir follows after. Then Katz quickly turns her head away and then a loud THWANG rings into the air. Vladmir falls to the ground completely out cold. Sivanna looks out the window to see what she hit. Katz stands over Vladmir as he lays there slowly coming to. Sivanna gasps.

"Oh, I am so sorry! I thought you were one of those crafty critters trying to sneak into the kitchen."

She looks down at her pan to see a faint dent in the pan's bottom. Vladmir sits up and groans. He holds his face in his hands. Katz leans over with her hands on her knees.

"Are you OK?"

Vladmir sniffs and gently rubs his nose.

"I'm good, nothing's broken."

Katz sighs in relief as Vladmir gets off the ground.

"We just wanted to see how things were going aaaannd hope to get something to eat?"

Sivanna disappears from the window and then pops back out again with a small plate of food.

"Here you go."

Katz walks up to the window and takes the plate. She waves good-bye and her and Vladmir go and sit down to eat. Katz takes a small skewer of meat. Oh how much she missed eating real food. She looks over at Vladmir who is just staring off into the distance. She holds the plate in front of him.

"Would you like a piece?"

"No, it is yours. I'm fine."

"It's OK if you take some."

She holds the plate out to him and he takes the small bread roll. Vladmir takes a bite out of the roll and Katz giggles.

"What?"

"I just think it's funny that I missed my birthday. I didn't realize I was in the castle that long. Now I'm here to celebrate with my family and friends."

Katz looks up to see Vladmir is facing away from her.

"Is there something wrong?"

He doesn't answer. She smells her breath and realizes what is bothering Vladmir. She stinks of garlic. She eats a mint leaf and drinks some water. She smells her breath again and looks back at Vladmir.

"Sorry, is that better?"

Vladmir turns around with relief on his face.

"I forgot you hate garlic so much."

"It is alright. Garlic just never agreed with me."

Then Katz just realizes something. If she doesn't tell her grandmother, most of the food will be cooked with garlic! Katz gives the plate to Vladmir and runs back to the kitchen. She jumps up to the window.

"Grandma! Grandma!"

Sivanna wipes sweat from her brow and walks over to the window.

"Yes, what is it dear?"

"Grandma, you can't cook with garlic!"

"Why?"

"Vladmir doesn't like it, he said it never agreed with him."

"Ooooh. Well at this point we can't just redo the meal so I will ask the cook if he can prepare something for him."

Sivanna walks back into the kitchen and finds the cook. She sees him busy taste-testing with Scott next to him.

"Now, Scott, I need you to continue to stir this slowly until the vegetables are well cooked."

The cook sees Sivanna signaling him over. He walks over to her and Scott listens on to the conversation secretively.

"Can you cook something without garlic?"

"Why?"

"My granddaughter's friend doesn't like garlic very much. I do believe she said it doesn't agree with him."

"Ahh, OK I will prepare a separate dish for him."

"Thank you."

Sivanna walks away and the cook comes back and checks on the stew. He takes the pot off the fire. Scott follows behind him. Scott smiles quietly to himself and takes a piece of garlic. *I knew it, he is a vampire.*

Everything is finally finished. The decorations are up, the food is cooked, and everyone is ready. They all gather around the fire pit and wait for the celebration to begin. A main table stretches across behind the fire where the Elders, Scott, Jack, Suki, Sivanna, and Vladmir sit. All the other villagers sit on the blankets that lie on the ground around the fire pit. A seat is left empty by Sivanna and Katz is nowhere to be seen. The head Elder stands.

"Welcome all to a wonderful celebration, to celebrate a special day. Katz, the granddaughter of Elder Sivanna, has come back to us. So today we celebrate her arrival and the day of her birth. Welcome home Katz!"

The crowd looks away from the fire and down an open path. A figure appears in the light of the fire. It is Katz. She is adorned in a beautiful dress of a pale blue with a thick white collar that wraps around her shoulders. At the end of the long sleeves and at the hem of the dress, a pale purple trim wraps all the way around. Then small silver trim and designs decorate the dress bringing out its beauty as it sparkles in the fire's light. Her long hair flows down her back and a pale blue headband sits atop her head. Katz's necklace glistens in the light upon her chest. She continues to walk down the path to her seat at the table. Jack's heart flutters as he watches Katz walk towards the table and Scott just smiles. Vladmir is in awe of her beauty but doesn't allow anyone else to notice. Katz stands next to the head Elder in the middle of the table.

"Katz, we welcome you and your friends to our humble village and all wish you a happy birthday."

They crowd cheers and happy birthdays ring from the crowd. Katz cheeks grow red and she smiles.

"Now let the feast begin!"

The cooks start to bring out the food and placing it onto tables towards the back of the crowd. Dish upon dish begin to line up and down the table. Once the tables were set the head cook comes up and signals the table where Katz and the rest sat to come up and eat. Before Valdmir could get up the head cook places a plate before him.

"Here this is for you. I was told you dislike garlic so this plate has none."

Vladmir bows his head to the cook and the cook walks away. So Vladmir sits and waits for the rest to receive their food. Katz is first to get food. Her eyes widen with anticipation and hunger. She takes a stone plate and begins to fill her plate with food. She takes legs of meat, roasted vegetables, and small bowl of stew, and couple of rolls. Then everyone else follows behind her. When she gets back to the table a cup of water sits. Once everyone sits they all dig in. The crowd's voices rise as they chat to one another. Katz digs into her plate of food and enjoys every moment of it. Finally real food! All she ever had at the castle was stale bread, water, tea, and a piece of fruit if she was lucky. She looks down to the right to see all the Elders talking amongst each other. Down to her left all of her friends and grandmother are eating. Scott is digging into his five small bowls of stew and a plate full of bread, Vladmir and Sivanna eat like normal civilized people, and Jack just eats like any other normal kid. Katz just smiles and continues to eat. Vladmir stands up and excuses himself from the table to go and get another roll. Scott watches as Vladmir walks away and quickly squeezes the juice from the garlic clove onto Vladmir's dish and goes back to eating. Vladmir comes back and starts to eat. He gets to the last bits of food on his dish when he begins to feel sick. His head starts to spin and his stomach starts to do loops. He closes his eyes and covers his mouth as a small burp escapes. He pushes his chair out.

"Excuse me for a moment."

Vladmir quickly walks around the bend of trees and disappears. Katz notices something is up.

"Excuse me Grandma, I am going to check on Vladmir."

"Ok, I hope everything is alright."

Katz walks around the bend to see Vladmir bent over some bushes. She approaches cautiously.

"Vladmir are you OK?"

As she reaches for his shoulder he vomits into the bushes. He holds himself with a tree and places one hand on his forehead. He shakes with a blank stare into the bushes, and then he pukes again.

"Vladmir what happened?!"

Vladmir takes a couple of shallow breaths and clears his throat. He slouches against a tree and falls to the ground. He holds his stomach and winces in pain.

"Yes, I will be fine. I just need to sit."

Katz kneels down and looks at Vladmir with worry.

"What happened?"

Vladmir starts to stand up quivering and pukes once more into the bushes. Then he slouches next to the tree again.

"Remember how I told you that garlic doesn't agree with me?"

"But it can't be! I told my grandma to get you a separate plate with no garlic on it."

Sivanna comes around the corner and notices what is going on.

"What happened?"

Katz looks up to Sivanna with worried eyes.

"Someone put garlic into Vladmir's food!"

"But I told the cook not to. How could have this happened?"

Vladmir just sits against the tree with eyes closed, holding his stomach. Sivanna kneels down and places a hand onto Vladmir's forehead.

"Vladmir are you going to be alright? Anything I can give you to help?"

"Yeah I will be fine after it passes."

Xolstice comes with a cup of bubbling water.

"I saw you guys where gone for awhile and I could see your "sick-to-my-stomach-face" a mile away. So, I brought you this to help you settle your stomach."

Xolstice hands Vladmir the cup and he looks at it in disgust.

"I promise it will help."

Vladmir drinks the cup down slowly and hands it back to Xolstice.

"Thank you."

Katz stands up.

"I thank you both for your help; I will meet back at the party in a moment."

Vladmir shakes his head.

"I won't keep you away from your celebration. Go Katz, I will be fine."

"Are you sure?"

"Yes."

Katz, Sivanna, and Xolstice all head back to the party. Katz looks back and worries for Vladmir. Now the sounds are distant and Vladmir can finally relax.

The party has ended and everyone is heading back to their homes to rest. Katz asks all the cooks to see if anyone accidently put garlic into Vladmir's dish. No one did and the head cook made sure of it. Katz sat on a log next to the fire pit and watches the fire fade away. Jack walks over and sits next to her.

"So what happened to him?"

Katz draws an invisible circle on the log next to her.

"Someone put garlic into Vladmir's dish and made him very ill. I just don't know who."

"Oh."

Then Jack realizes something. Vampires hate garlic! Scott put garlic in Vladmir's dish! Jack hugs Katz and then rubs her on the shoulder.

"He will be fine, don't worry yourself too much."

"Thanks Jack. I'm going to go check on him."

Then Katz walks over to where she saw Vladmir last. Jack stands up and marches back to his hut where

Scott went to settle for the night. Katz turns the corner and sees that Vladmir is no longer there. She heads over to his hut to see if he is there. When she gets there, Vladmir is asleep on the cot. She sighs as her heart relaxes. She wants to go in but she doesn't want to disturb him so she quietly walks away.

"Good Night Vladmir."

Then she walks back to her grandma's hut and rests for the night.

Jack walks up to the hut, opens the door, and quietly closes the door. Scott looks up to see Jack is very angry. Jack walks over and pushes Scott in the chest so he hits the back wall.

"Why would you do that Scott? Why did you put garlic into Vladmir's food?"

Scott couldn't get words out of his mouth.

"You could have killed him! You made Katz very upset! I don't like seeing her upset!"

They are both now face to face both giving one another an angry look.

"I wasn't thinking. I just wanted to..."

Jack's eyes narrow.

"YOU STILL THINK HE IS A VAMPIRE!! Scott I have told you vampires don't exist!"

Scott cowers and Jack relaxes a bit because he could feel himself getting too worked up.

"Scott, being badly affected by garlic doesn't make anyone a vampire. He may fit the description but it doesn't make him one."

"I know."

"You know what you have to do tomorrow, right?"

"Yes."

Scott holds his knees that are under the covers. He turns his head away from Jack. Jack sits next to Scott.

"Look, I'm sorry for getting angry but you hurt Katz. Just remember to think before you act."

"Ok."

Then they both get into their sheets and go to sleep. Jack turns to Scott's direction.

"Just leave the vampire stuff out of it."

Chapter 15

Scott slowly walks up to Katz's and Sivanna's hut. A knot tightly wound itself in his stomach. He approaches the doorway to see Katz and Sivanna talking. He knocks on the wall of the doorway. They both look in his direction.

"Hi, ah, I need to talk to you guys about something."

Katz smiles and Sivanna allows him in. He sits in the chair across from them, his head down, and twiddling with his thumbs. He looks up with worried eyes.

"So, what did you need to talk to us about Scott?"

"I did something….last night…"

Katz and Sivanna look with concern. Sweat begins to fall from Scott's brow.

"I….I….put the garlic in Vladmir's food…..last night…"

Sivanna gasps and Katz's eyes fill with tears. Katz stands up.

"HOW COULD YOU! YOU COULD HAVE KILLED HIM! Scott, why?!"

Scott looks up to see tears falling down Katz's face then her face grows to anger.

"WHY?!"

"I...just...wanted....to play.....a prank..."

Katz stares in shock.

"A PRANK?! A PRANK?!"

Scott stands up.

"I DIDN'T KNOW HE DIDN'T LIKE GARLIC! I WASN'T THINKING AND I KNOW THAT!"

Scott falls back into his chair and curls up hiding his face.

"I'm sorry.... I.. didn't know."

Katz relaxes and takes in deep rapid breaths. Sivanna touches Scott's shoulder.

"We accept your apology but you need to apologize to Vladmir too."

"I accept his apology."

They all look up to the doorway to see Vladmir standing there. Scott turns away. Katz jumps for joy.

"You're OK!"

Sivanna stands up.

"So how are you feeling?"

"I am fine just can't eat anything yet. My stomach is still sensitive."

Scott looks down at his fidgeting feet.

"I'm sorry Vladmir. I didn't know."

Vladmir just smiles.

"It's alright just be careful who you prank next time."

Scott looks up and smiles. He stands up and shakes hands with Vladmir and turns and hugs Katz. He waves good-bye and heads back outside.

Scott and Jack are out on the training field practicing their fighting skills. Suki is just there to heal if anyone gets hurt. After sparring for awhile they sit in the cool grass to relax. Scott just smiles and holds up three fingers.

"That's three to two."

"Yeah, one of them I got something in my eye so that doesn't count."

"Pfft, yeah right."

Scott, Jack, and Suki just laugh. Jack looks about him and yet again spots Vladmir and this time with Katz. He is training her with a wooden sword. Katz just laughs and giggles every time she hits Vladmir. Jack continues to watch them as the volley shots back and forth at each other. He grips the grass tighter and tighter every time he gets a hit on Katz. Then they both sit down and relax after a good sparring. Jack stands up.

"I am just going to get some more water."

Scott waves him on and Suki just waves. Jack quietly sneaks behind some trees and bushes a few feet behind Katz and Vladmir. Something in his gut keeps telling him that something is wrong with this guy. He takes his dagger and points it to Vladmir. *I want to know the past of Vladmir.*

"Verrass."

The dagger fires a stabbing pain up his arm and into his head. Jack falls holding the sides of his head. He feels the presence next to whisper the story of Vladmir.

Long ago a fierce being threaten the land. Under his power was Vladmir. With the wave of its hand he became the Nightling and terrorized the village and almost killed everyone at the village. Then the Nightling and the being were banished forever in darkness.

Jack sits back up with his heart pounding in his chest. He looks over at Vladmir. Thoughts race through his head. Can all this be true? He knew there was something up about Vladmir but this? Jack's head fumbles with thoughts trying to connect the dots. How? Why? When? So many confusing thoughts just became a melted mess. Jack gets up and shakes his head. May be he heard the spirit wrong and waited for the thoughts to settle. So he takes his dagger and heads back over to Scott and Suki. He points his dagger at Scott.

"You up for another sparring match?"

"You're on!"

They take their stance and start to spar once more. Jack hopes a little more sparring will take his mind off the subject.

Late at night Jack rustles in his sheets as nightmares ravage his dreams. He tosses and turns and abruptly wakes up. He breathes in heavily as sweat beads down his face. The images from his mind are blurry and mixed together making no sense. He relaxes himself and goes back to sleep hoping the nightmares stay away. In the morning Jack wakes up and feels like he had no sleep at all last night. He looks over to see Scott is already out of bed, so that means he has slept in more than usual. He gets up and heads out for the day.

All day his mind keeps losing focus on what he is supposed to be doing, lingering on Vladmir being the Nightling. His mind just couldn't comprehend that. He keeps passing it off as just jealousy towards Vladmir, so all day he tries to keep his mind off the subject. He helps Suki with chores, spars with Scott, and even tries to take a walk in the woods to help clear his mind. Jack did his best to keep his distance from Vladmir hoping the thoughts will stay away. Then night draws near and everyone heads off to bed.

The nightmares rage in his head. Pictures of the Nightling and the being flash in his mind, sometimes chasing him. He watches as the Nightling destroys the village and kills its people. In his dreams Jack tries to scream and warn them but nothing came from him. He yells out with no avail. Then the Nightling spots him. It walks up to Jack on all fours slowly and cautiously. The Nightling's shape blurs and grows revealing a tall dark mass with glowing red eyes. Without any warning the figure charges him taking over every part of his body.

He could feel the cold evil slither under his skin changing him. He runs towards a puddle of water and looks. Staring back at him is the Nightling. He tries to back away but something holds him there. Then the Nightling jumps out from the puddle at him and screams a blood curdling scream. Jack awakens with Scott at his side. Jack curls up and places his head on his knees feeling his heart hitting against his chest.

"Jack, are you alright? You sounded like you were having one nasty dream."

Jack looks up at Scott with sleepless eyes.

"Yeah, I'll be fine it was just a nightmare."

Jack walks over to Sivanna's hut to see if she is there. He peeks into the door to see her there sipping a cup of hot tea. He knocks on the doorway.

"Sivanna can I ask you a question?"

"Sure Jack, please, come sit."

Jack sits on the chair across from her.

"Sivanna I had this question bugging my mind for awhile. What happens if you don't believe what the goddess tells you when you use the power of the dagger?"

Sivanna just smiles.

"Nothing should happen. The goddess understands if you doubt her and will not force her thoughts on you. She knows that someday you may believe it or not."

Jack stands up.

"Thanks."

Jack walks out the door and heads towards the training grounds. When he gets there he sees Vladmir and Katz sparring. Then a sudden cold dread feeling consumes his body. A thought crosses his mind. *If he is the Nightling he could hurt Katz! That thing can kill with no mercy!* Then the images from his dreams flash into his mind and a voice calling out to him. *You must believe or the ones you love will die.* Then anger swells inside of him. He would do anything to keep Katz safe. So he sits and waits for Vladmir to be alone. Finally Katz leaves and Vladmir heads into the forest and Jack follows. Vladmir enters the forest and walks into a clearing watching the creatures skitter by across the ground playfully chasing one another. Then he hears something big behind him. It is Jack, with a dagger in hand.

"Vladmir you must leave!"

Vladmir watches cautiously.

"Why?"

"Because Katz knows your secret, who you really are."

Vladmir's jaw drops as the cold realization hits him. How could Katz know? So he tries to act casual.

"What secret do you speak of?"

Jack gets into a defensive stance.

"Don't toy with me Vladmir! You know what secret I speak of! I want you to leave NOW!"

Vladmir picks up the closest branch and takes his stance. Jack begins to breathe heavily and shaky. Vladmir tightly grips the branch.

"I told her! I will not let you hurt her or anyone in this village!"

Jack comes charging at Vladmir and strikes first. With each hit Jack left small indentations in the branch. Pieces of wood fly here and there as Vladmir blocks Jack's attacks. Valdmir takes his branch and swings it under Jack's feet knocking him over. Jack jumps back up and charges once more. He hits faster and faster and finally breaks the branch into splintering pieces. Vladmir drops the pieces and dodges Jack's attacks. Jack backs away from Vladmir leaving a good distance between them. They glare at one another waiting for the next move. Then Jack just vanishes into thin air. Vladmir quickly looks around to see where Jack may appear. Then from above Jack falls with the dagger in hand, ready to kill. Vladmir falls back on his hands and pushes forward kicking Jack square in the chest. Jack flies across the ground and hits a tree. The dagger falls out of his hand just feet from him. Vladmir walks cautiously to Jack's motionless body. A deep, cold laughter surrounds them. The air grows heavy and cold and everything darkens. Jack's arms, legs, and body are pulled upwards as if hanging from puppet strings. Vladmir looks up and Jack's head hangs low so his face is not seen. Vladmir tries to see his face.

"Jack?"

Jack lowers to just above the ground but just high enough to be at Vladmir's eye level. Vladmir waits and listens as the silence hangs between them. Then a cold hand grips his heart and causes him to fall on one knee as if the air is knocked out of him. He looks back up to see Jack's face but it is not his. His face is twisted with big sharp teeth and glaring red eyes. His mouth twisted into an evil grin. A soft hiss slithers from his dagger-like teeth. Vladmir gasps.

"Nightmare."

Jack just laughs.

"Ah you finally figure it out."

Vladmir backs away from Jack.

"But....I..."

"You thought I was going to use you to get here? Such stupidity. That would have made it too obvious. You wouldn't have stayed if I came through you so I needed someone else, a different source. As I watched, a child I see, filled with uncontrollable anger and jealousy, a very useful source, easily taken."

Vladmir takes his stance and grows angry.

"You let him go!"

Jack smiles.

"He is so much like you. Anger so easily taken advantage of. A weakness you both share."

"Let him go Nightmare! He has nothing to do with this!"

Jacks laughs.

"Oh not so, he has much more to do with this than you think."

Jack's face returns to normal and a horrified face looks down at Vladmir, his chest rapidly rising and falling with his panicked breathing.

"Vladmir? What's going on? Why am I up here? Why can't I..."

The strings holding Jack begin to pull and bend his body into painful positions. His arms go above his head and begin to fall back. His feet follow suit as if both his hands and feet were trying to touch. Jack screams out in pain as his back is pushed more and more to its limit. The bones began to quietly crack but not snap. A figure stands in front of the forest waiting for Jack to come back out. Suki paces outside the forest and hears the bloodcurdling screams. She watches as the forest in front of her grows dark and all living things in it run out. The creatures flee in terror, squealing and chattering; an icy cold breeze brush passed her face and fills her with fear. She slowly backs away from the forest in terror of what may lie within the trees. She runs back to the village hoping for whomever to help her. Vladmir steps into the shadows and lands in the trees just behind Jack. He leaps out and brings Jack to the ground. Vladmir stands and Jack remains motionless on the ground.

Suddenly Jack flies back up his eyes glowing red and a face of pure anger disfiguring his face. Vladmir takes him by the throat and holds him up against the tree. Jack struggles to get free and Vladmir continues to hold. Vladmir glares straight into Jack's eyes.

"You will not hurt this boy!"

Then Jack stops moving and looks back into Vladmir's eyes.

"So be it."

A black mist melts away from Jack and creeps under Vladmir's skin. Veins of black grow down his arm and further covering his body. They pulsate as more and more of the mass enters his body. His body grows cold and his consciousness begins to fade. He tries to fight it then everything goes black and Jack falls limp. Jack awakens to see Vladmir pinning him against a tree and unable to breathe. He looks up to see that what is standing in front of him is not Vladmir. In his place is a dark figure with pitch black eyes and an evil twisted face. It smiles as its grip gets tighter and tighter around Jack's neck. Jack reaches for his neck trying to pry open its grip. He gasps for air and hears the rustling of leaves behind him. He looks off to his left to see Suki and Katz appear from the forest. Katz and Suki stare in terror at the scene they see before them. Suki grabs Katz's hand.

"I get more help. Get Sivanna!"

Suki runs back into the forest as fast as she can back to the village. Katz stands in fear and shock of what stands before her. She looks down to see Jack's dagger and picks it up. She holds it up with two shaking hands and points it towards Vladmir.

"Let him go."

The dark figure looks over at Katz and releases Jack from its grip. Jacks falls to the ground as the figure turns and slowly heads towards Katz. She takes a quivering defensive stance.

"Vladmir I am warning you! Don't come any closer!"

He continues to come closer and closer until only a few feet stand between him and Katz. Katz begins to cry.

"Vladmir this is not you! Snap out of this! What has gotten into you? Vladmir! Please, stop!"

He stops just a couple of feet in front of Katz. The dagger sits out in front of Katz just in front of her chest.

Her heart pounds, tears flow, and her body shivers in fear.

"Please, Vladmir, I don't want to hurt you."

He looks right into her eyes and just smiles. Katz's eyes grow wide in fear. Then Vladmir flies straight at her and she closes her eyes. The coldness goes away, light comes through the trees, and the presence is gone. Katz opens her eyes and looks up. She feels something warm covering her fingertips. Her heart drops. She removes her hands revealing that she has stabbed Vladmir, straight into his heart. Vladmir regains his consciousness and feels his chest. He sees a dagger protruding from his chest and looks up to see Katz's face wet with tears and her fingers covered in blood. He reaches out to her and she backs away. She shakes her head and looks over at Jack and runs to him. He turns and tries to speak but nothing comes out. He takes a step towards them. Katz turns away and cradles Jack's head in her arms.

"No! Stay away from us!"

"But Katz...."

"NO! Why did you do this Vladmir? Why?"

Footsteps are heard running through the forest. Vladmir turns around and gasps and grips at his chest. In front of him stands Sivanna with her hand on the dagger's hilt. He looks at her as she pushes the dagger all the way through and out the other side. Katz watches as he falls to the ground and buries her face into Jack's chest and just cries. Sivanna and a couple of the villagers came up to Jack and Katz. Suki takes Katz around the shoulders and leads her out of the forest. The two villagers make a makeshift stretcher and carry Jack out of the forest. Sivanna walks back over to Vladmir. She kneels down beside him and flips him over. She takes hold of the dagger and pulls it out. Vladmir gasps for air as he places a hand over his wound. He sits up as Sivanna stands.

"You will now leave this village. You will never be allowed back and never to see my granddaughter again."

Vladmir takes hold of Sivanna's hand.

"Please, before I go, let me show you what truly happened that night."

Sivanna stares off into an endless abyss and images of the terrible night flash back into her mind.

Chapter 16

Nothing but black is seen as the images begin to show themselves to her. Faintly, in the black, colors begin to light the darkness. They reveal themselves as a door of light opening up in the darkness. Sivanna's mind enters the door that leads to a room. As she steps in the image of herself changes into a young black haired girl in an elegant red dress with a beautiful masquerade mask. The mask itself is red with gold beading outlining the mask and eyes and there are three large feathers, two black and one red, sticking out from the right side from a scarlet gem. She looks about to see the room that she stands in is a magnificent library. Books line up and down the walls and a window sits behind with a seat built right in. Then her body walks towards the door and opens it. She turns right and heads down the hallway. Loud noises of chatter and music begin to fill the air. As she comes to the end of the hallway she is now at the top of a grand staircase. A deep red carpet flows down the center of the stairs and the railings gleam with their beautiful carvings in the light. On the stairs and in the main foyer people dance and laugh while talking amongst each other. Everyone is dressed in beautiful gowns and tuxedos and everyone is wearing masks, some just plain and simple and others full of glitter and sparkling gems. Sivanna begins to walk down the stairs and the crowd quiets down. Down in the center of the crowd stands a figure with a long black cape with a tall collar, white shirt, a black hat with one red feather, a gold sun-like mask, black pants, and a red vest that sparkles in the lamp's light. He raises his hands.

"Everyone I welcome you to my humble home on this wonderful night."

It is Vladmir. She has never seen him so happy. She stops midway on the stairs and listens.

"I thank you all for coming to come celebrate a wondrous occasion."

Vladmir turns and takes someone from the crowd. It is a beautiful young lady who is wearing a gorgeous blue dress, from the waist down the dress flairs out with little sparkles glittering in the light. The top is strapless and hugs tightly around her chest and is a deep blue silken color. Similar colored gloves cover all the way up just past her elbows. A see-through dark blue shawl hangs around her shoulders. Her hair hangs down around her shoulders in loose curls. Upon her face she wears a silver-pearl colored mask with silver studs outlining the mask and eyes. Small silver detailing fill in the spaces and two long pieces of see-through cloth hang from either side with small silver stars hidden within. She smiles as she stands next to Vladmir. Vladmir holds her hands to his face and kisses them.

"As in my family tradition, we are here to celebrate something very special. Today we celebrate the day I first met this beautiful young lady a year ago. Today we celebrate our one year anniversary of being together!"

The crowd cheers and Vladmir picks up the girl around the waist and twirls her in a circle. He brings her close, kisses her, and she smiles. Sivanna's heart fills with joy at the love between these two individuals. Then the music starts up again and everyone joins in a circle. Sivanna races down the stairs to join in. Vladmir and the girl stand in the center.

"Now for our first game of the night we shall dance. On the floor you will see two red tiles."

He points down to the floor to two red tiles spaced far apart from one another.

"We will all line up in a pattern of woman, gentleman, woman, and so on. We will dance in a circle and when the music stops those who stand closest to the red tiles shall dance with one another. The musicians will play a song and the two must dance and then will start again once more."

Everyone gathers in a circle and starts dancing in a circle as the music plays. The tune is fun and uplifting and everyone starts moving faster and faster. The red tiles become blurs on the floor and everyone just laughs. Then the music stops. Everyone looks to see who stands in front of the red tiles. An older gentleman stands at one and a young woman at the other. They meet in middle and bow to one another and the music starts once more. They dance a fast waltz in the center, twirling round and round. The music ends, they bow, and the crowd cheers and once again begins to twirl in a circle to the music. The music stops and now two gentlemen stand at either tile. They meet in the middle, shrug their shoulders and dance to the fast waltz, twirling in circles. As soon as the men rejoin the circle then the group meet in the middle and reach for the center and back out once more. Then all of them form an arch and the first two on the left side run down the center and join at the end. Just happiness and laughter fills the air. It is Sivanna's turn and she runs down the center with a man and they just laugh. Then Vladmir notices chefs bringing out food and filling glasses with wine. He signals to the crowd.

"My friends, dinner is served."

They all enter the ballroom in which they converted half of it into a dining hall. Everyone one sat down and the gentlemen all pull the chairs out for the women to allow them to sit. Vladmir pulls out a chair for the young girl and he sits next to her. In small groups they all came up to the tables and picked out their meal and towards the end a chef stands by a ham that he carves when someone asks. The smells were just as wonderful as the food tasted. Sivanna looks over at the couples who chat amongst themselves giggling every now and then. Once dinner is over everyone heads out to the foyer and relaxes with a glass of wine. Sivanna takes a seat on the stairs and sips from her glass. Vladmir walks up to her, looks behind, and looks back at Sivanna.

"Can I trust you with a secret?"

Sivanna is caught off guard and just nods. He takes her by the hand and leads her to the library. He closes the door behind them. Sivanna looks around nervous of what may happen, and Vladmir walks up to her pulling a small box from his pocket. He pops open a box to reveal a beautiful sapphire ring. The ring had a sapphire blue crescent moon and two diamonds sit on either side, two towards the top and two towards the bottom. The silver ring that holds the moon starts as a whole band but then splits into two on either side then connecting to each diamond. The blue of the sapphire glows in the light. Sivanna places her hand over her mouth. Vladmir looks with excited eyes.

"Do you think she will like it?"

Sivanna looks at the ring and up at Vladmir and smiles.

"She will love it."

Vladmir gives her a hug, places the box back in his pocket, and leads back out to the foyer. Everyone is just sitting around chatting with one another. Vladmir leaves Sivanna at the stairs and she sits. Then the young lady comes and sits next to her. She looks about and pulls a small black box from behind her. She turns her back to the crowd.

"I got this for Vladmir. Do you think he will like it?"

She opens the box to see a single rose with a blue ribbon tied onto its stem. The flower itself is a beautiful pale bluish purple that seems to sparkle in the light. It also gently glows with a pale blue-whitish light. Sivanna goes to reach for the rose and the lady closes the box and looks to Sivanna for an answer.

"So?"

"He will love it."

"Yes, I thought so. We grew this in the garden together and it's the first one to bloom and he doesn't know yet."

She gets up and heads into the crowd. Vladmir gets the crowd's attention once more.

"Everyone may I have your attention. Before we end the night, I have a gift to present to my love."

Vladmir reaches for his box when the young lady quickly pulls out her box. She looks with excitement.

"May I go first?"

Vladmir nods and reaches for the black box with the red ribbon. He unties the ribbon and opens the lid. He reaches in and pulls out the rose with the blue ribbon on it. He reaches out and gives the girl a great big hug and kisses her on the cheek.

"I love it dear!"

"It is the first one to bloom."

Vladmir places the rose into his vest so the flower sticks out. He reaches into his pocket and pulls out the small box.

"Now here is mine."

He hands the box out to her and she gently takes it with caution and curiosity. She opens the lid to reveal a beautiful blue ring. She places a hand over her mouth and jumps on Vladmir and hugs him.

"Oh Vladmir, it's beautiful! It even has a sapphire moon stone."

Vladmir takes the box and removes the ring from the box. He takes the ring and places it on her finger; the young lady examines the ring and just smiles.

"Oh thank you."

They hug each other once more and Sivanna's happiness is cut short. A deep cold chill runs up her spine and she looks around. A fierce wind flies through the room and extinguishes the lights. Everyone stops and looks around. Then something makes them all look at the top of the stairs. There a dark floating mass levitates at the top. The crowd watches waiting for the mass to do something. The mass starts to grow and the room gets darker. Two massive arms shoot out of either side and surround the crowd as they gasp and duck out of the way. The arms slowly go back to the form and it lifts its head. Upon its head sat a hat with red eyes and sharp teeth. The face of the figure reveals itself to have identical glowing red eyes and razor sharp teeth. Vladmir and the young lady hold close waiting for what the figure may do. Vladmir stands in front of the young lady and looks up to the figure.

"Who are you?"

A sinister chuckle echoes about the room, then the figure smiles. It throws its arms into the air and the room fills with fire. The crowd screams as they all rush for any exit they could find. Sivanna watches in terror as the room is engulfed in flames. A gentleman from the party takes her by the arm and pulls her out of the castle. Then Sivanna's mind spins causing the images to blur and then everything becomes clear. She is running and pulling someone behind her. She looks towards her left and sees her reflection and it is not her at all. She is seeing through Vladmir's eyes. He looks back to see the young lady, very frightened and tears coming from underneath her mask. Vladmir continues to run and then something stops them in their tracks, a force that keeps them from running away.

"Vladmir, why can we not move?"

"I am not sure."

Then the force starts to slowly pull them back to the foyer. The young lady screams as she grips tighter onto Vladmir's hand. Vladmir reaches out and grabs the doorway. His fingers slide as the force pulls and pulls. Then the two lovers fly back to the foyer.

"VLADMIR!"

Vladmir lands on the staircase and the young lady falls to the foyer floor and lays motionless. Vladmir gets up and notices she is not moving. Sivanna and Vladmir both begin to fill with rage and anger. They look at the top of the stairs and see the figure before them. They both scream out.

"Who are you and why are you destroying my home?!"

The evil figure doesn't say anything. It reaches out for the young lady and picks her up and holds her over the fire. It smiles as it slowly lowers her into the flames. Vladmir runs up the stairs but the figure sends its other hand into his chest. Vladmir stops cold in his tracks. The figure lowers its head so it and Vladmir are face to face. Sivanna's heart sinks as she feels the power take over. Vladmir looks into its face.

"What do you want?"

"You."

"Why?"

"I need a host."

"A host for what?"

The figure begins to lower the lady into the fire, the flames reaching for her face. Vladmir reaches out.

"No!"

Vladmir reaches out and tries to hit the mass but just goes right through it. In anger and rage he just keeps on trying to attack the mass. Then both Vladmir and Sivanna feel the death cold grip wrap around their heart. Vladmir falls to his knees as each beat of his heart hurts.

"Take what you need from me but don't harm her."

He looks over at her as she lies limp. The figure smiles and pulls an orb from thin air. He holds the orb in front of Vladmir. The orb begins to pulsate. Vladmir watches the orb and feels a cold emptiness fill his chest. The orb begins to pulsate and echo the sound of a heart beating. Vladmir gasps and grabs his chest as it begins to freeze. His hair goes from black to white and his eyes change to a deep red. The figure releases him, drops the lady, and the fire extinguishes. Smoke swirls into a big cloud and shrinks until it no longer exists. Vladmir gets up and runs towards the girl but falls. His body refuses to get up and he just lies there reaching for her. The figure floats over to the young girl and picks her up and disappears. Vladmir clumsily gets up and looks around. He runs outside and looks and something makes him turn to the forest behind his castle. He runs to the forest edge when he is stopped by a scream. A blood-curdling scream that echoes throughout the forest. Vladmir falls to his knees and tears fall quietly down his face. Sivanna could hear his thoughts echo in her head. *It said it would bring no harm to her. I did what it said. Now she is gone.* The figure reappears before him and he doesn't even look up. The images swirl once again and now Sivanna is standing next to Vladmir. The figure reaches a hand above Vladmir and a thick black cloud swarms around him. Vladmir yells out as the sounds of cracking and breaking bones emanates from the cloud. Then everything goes silent. Sivanna backs away as she could feel a very dark presence stand before her. A black creature jumps out of the cloud and screams into the night, the dark figure chuckles and points out and into the forest.

"Go forth, my Nightling, and head to Azmala and destroy the bloodline to the moon goddess."

The Nightling falls onto all fours and runs into the forest and barges through the doors leading into the world of Azmala. Sivanna tries to look away but she knows she must face that night once again. Everything goes black and Sivanna stands alone in the darkness. Then a voice echoes around her. *I know you have seen this event before but I must complete the story for you to remember it.* Sivanna nods her head and looks off into a distance. A small speck of light stands at a distance and quiet screams of terror come from it. Sivanna takes a step towards it and then she is completely immersed into the image. All around her are burning homes, lifeless bodies, children crying, screaming, and people running in terror. A mother and her child runs past her and the Nightling came quickly behind them. A fellow villager stands in the way and is struck in the heart with its tail. The villager falls and shrivels up as the poison goes through his veins. He is able to scream once more before falling over to join the other bodies that lie across the ground. The mother and child got away and the Nightling goes after its next victim. Sivanna walks over the bodies and follows the Nightling. She begins to shake and tears grow warm in her eyes. She knows where she is at now. She turns the corner seeing her daughter and a young girl running hand in hand as the creature chases them. A man came in between them.

"Go, I will deal with this creature."

They nod their heads and continue to run. The man brings out a sword and waits for the creature. As the Nightling approaches, it slows down and begins to pace around the man. The man snarls at the creature and strikes only to see the Nightling is not there. He pulls his sword from the earth and looks about him waiting for the creature to attack. From behind the creature appears and latches onto his back. The man drops his sword as the Nightling sinks its teeth deep into his neck. The man falls to his knees and the Nightling pushes off the man and leaves him laying face down on the earth. Sivanna looks on down the path to see her daughter hide the young girl behind some rubble. Then she takes the stone from her necklace and the dagger from her waist. She places the stone into the dagger and it grows into a glowing sword. As the Nightling lunges for her she strikes the Nightling across the chest and sends it flying over her. The Nightling gets up on all fours and looks down to see green glowing blood ooze from its chest. It shrieks into the night and races back into the forest. The young girl cheers but then her cheer falls to tears as Sivanna's daughter falls. Sivanna looks to see herself running up to her daughter and the young girl following behind. She sees herself examine her daughter and finds a small cut across her arm. She has been struck by the Nightling's tail. The young girl falls to her knees next to Sivanna's daughter. Her daughter reaches for her hand.

"Bring her to me, I may not survive long."

The other Sivanna squeezes her hand and brings the young girl over to her daughter. Her daughter sits up in front of the sobbing kneeling girl before her. She takes her thumb and presses on her forehead, once on each shoulder, and once on the heart. She takes both of the young girl hands in hers. A small white light glows in between their hands and Sivanna's daughter falls and the young girl watches silently as her fingers slip from hers. She starts grabbing out to her and Sivanna takes her by the arm and pulls her away. They disappear in the darkness of the forest. Sivanna slowly walks up to her daughter's body. She kneels down beside her and gently strokes her cheek. She brushes her hair away from her face and waterfalls come from her eyes. Her heart aches with so much grief that it begins to hurt. She had to relive her daughter's death once more. She reaches for her hand but then she disappears with everything around her. Now she stands in the trees at the forest's edge where the tallest hill lies. At the top the evil being from before stands and a small black dot slowly crawls up the hill. The being looks over to see the Nightling, who is wounded, grovel at its feet. The being throws the Nightling off into the distance. It lays there for only a moment and it changes back to Vladmir. A force slowly drags the unconscious Vladmir up the hill. The being places a hand over him. His body twitches as it begins to change. The being lifts its hand to reveal Radaris standing before him, his face hidden by his cloak. Off to Sivanna's left the White Witches appear out of the forest and head to the hill. The White Witches cast the spell and everything goes white. Sivanna feels a force pull her back away from the light and back to where she began, with Vladmir holding her hand. Vladmir stands and leaves Sivanna kneeling in the wet grass, her horror-stricken sad eyes staring into an endless abyss. As Valdmir approaches the forest he looks back to see Sivanna looking back. He lowers his head and turns into the forest and vanishes. The forest grows quiet so only small insects make their simple music. Sivanna stands up and rubs her shoulders and wipes the tears from her eyes and heads out of the forest.

Vladmir approaches a clearing and looks out to see the last of the sun's light. He walks over to an old tree and sits down in front of it, every last feeling of hope gone from him, he just stares at the stars. Without looking he could feel Nightmare's presence as it approaches. A sinister chuckle echoes in Vladmir's ears as Hat plops near him. It lets out with a nasty sarcastic laugh as Nightmare raises its hand over Vladmir. Valdmir continues to look up and closes his eyes and is enveloped in a dark cloud-like mass. Bones break and his life falls to pieces, all life dies around him, and the wind stops. Once again the Nightling rises with its blood-curdling screams echoing into the night. Nightmare brings a cage in front of the Nightling. Inside, trapped behind bars, lies a white bird. On the tips of its great wings and tail is a red-golden color that shines in the light. Up its long neck are four rings of shining golden-red and long thin feathers stretch from its face starting from a bright yellow and ending in a bright red, and its orange and black beak squawking in anger and a garnet red gem on its chest. Nightmare smiles.

"Now the sun will never rise again leaving this world in darkness!"

Chapter 17

As Sivanna gets closer to the village she notices the sky starting to darken with low clouds. The clouds begin to swirl above the hill where it all began and yet no wind blew past her. She starts to run towards the village. Sivanna runs into the hut where all the head Elders are sitting around a small fire.

"Elders it is happening again! We must get everyone to safety now."

The Elders stand and the eldest comes to Sivanna.

"We must hurry, it will be here soon."

Sivanna runs to her hut and finds Katz, Scott, and Jack, who is still unconscious, inside. Scott looks out the window.

"What is going on out there?"

"We need to get you three to safety; there is no time for questions."

"He's back isn't he?"

Sivanna looks at Katz and sits down next to Katz and hugs her around the shoulders.

"Yes."

Jack begins to stir and mumble something under his breath. Katz reaches for a damp towel and pats his forehead.

"Katz.....night.....Vl....bad....hmm.."

Jack's eyes pop wide open and he sits up looking about himself. He looks around to see Sivanna, Katz, and Scott watching him but where is Vladmir? Jack tries to stand up but his head begins to spin and he sits back down.

"What happened? Where is he?"

Katz turns away and begins to cry quietly.

"He's gone, he won't hurt you no more."

Katz stands up, walks out the door, and Jack's gaze just follows her. Scott just shrugs his shoulders and looks back out the window. Jack looks out the window from the bed to see dark swirling clouds speeding fast. He stands up and walks towards the window.

"Why is it so dark?"

Sivanna gets up and joins them at the window.

"Your training will now be put to the test. He will come and this time with full force. He will leave nothing behind."

Sivanna takes both Jack's and Scott's hands and holds them in hers.

"We must get the villagers to safety and protect this village of what is to come. I pray for the both of you to be safe and may the goddess watch over you."

The people of the village gather what they can and head for a secret shelter that is underground. The women and children stayed together while the men helped fortify the village above ground. The men bound spear heads to staffs and sharpened stone swords. Others covered their bodies in tough leather armor. Katz, Jack, Scott, Xolstice, and Suki put on armor too while Sivanna puts on her Elder's robe. Along the edge of the village each Elder summons great power. They bring the earth up making a wall rise from the ground, branches of trees intertwine with one another over the great walls, and thorny vines weave a deadly net in front of the walls. Now they all stand around the great fire pit. The Elders send Xolstice, Suki, and some men to guard the entrance to the shelter. The rest of the men fan out in front while the Elders, Sivanna, Katz, Scott, and Jack stand in back. Now they wait for him to come. Everyone looks about themselves in every direction looking for anything moving in the distance. No birds sang, no insects chirped, and no life wandered in and out of the trees. Katz looks over to see one of the Elders next to her starting to cry.

"Elder, why are you crying?"

"My worst fear has come true. There is no sun to light this darkness."

The rest look to the sky to see not one stream of light penetrate the clouds, when the clouds part only a dark sky and little stars shine through. The sun has not risen to its mighty post in the sky. Katz looks back at the crying Elder.

"Why hasn't the sun risen?"

"He has taken hold and captured the Bird of Light so this land has fallen to darkness. A beautiful bird would cross the sky bringing the light of the sun behind it and take it away when the night is nigh. Now we are all in darkness."

A thick, white fog bleeds through the openings of the trees and slithers across the ground covering everyone's feet. The men draw their swords, Jack, Scott, Sivanna, and Katz pull out their daggers, and the Elders take hold of their staffs. The air grows ice cold and dark whispers quietly echo in the night. Everyone looks around frantically trying to find the source. Then a great black shadow covers them. They look up to see a great mass standing before them. It stands taller than any tree and doesn't move. Everyone waits anxiously to see what will happen. A quiet, deep, evil laughter creeps into everyone's mind. Katz looks up to see two pairs of glaring red eyes looking down upon them and two sharp-toothed dagger-like smiles grinning back. A great black hand pulls away from the figure and strikes down the center of the wall in front of the village causing the ground to shake. Another hand pulls away and strikes down next to the other and rips an opening in the trees. The wall crumbles and the branches splinter into a million pieces, as the hands pull apart a great swarm of ragdoll like creatures charge through the opening screeching and howling into the night. The figure reaches to the air and lightening bursts from the skies and strike down in front of the men. In the flashes of lightening a small creature flies high into the sky, its dark blue skin reflecting in the light and its bright red eyes glaring down. It lands down in front of the charging creatures and they stop. The creature stands upon its hind legs and shrieks sending chills down the villagers' spines. The creature falls down on all fours and charges into the village with ragdolls behind it. The men raise their weapons and charge forward. The Elders stay behind near the fire pit and throw fire balls at the enemy. Sivanna, Jack, Scott, and Katz follow behind the men ready to attack. The two sides collide into one another sending the ringing sound of blades meeting claws echo into the darkness. With one strike to a ragdoll they fall disappearing into the darkness. Katz, Jack, and Scott stand back to back as the ragdolls close in. Jack strikes out and kills one of the ragdolls and Katz and Scott join in. Each of them takes a turn taking down a ragdoll and avoiding their slashing claws. Katz slices one right down the middle and freezes when she hears a blood-curdling scream. She looks up to see the Nightling falling towards her. She is paralyzed by its gaze and cannot move. Just before the Nightling strikes Jack tackles the Nightling from the side and sends them both flying back into the crowd. Scott shakes Katz to awaken her from the trance.

"You okay?"

"Yeah."

She reaches behind him and blocks an attack. Scott ducks and turns around stabbing the creature in the stomach and it vanishes in a puff of black. Scott gives Katz a high-five and continues to fight.

The two break apart as they smack straight into a tree. The Nightling flies off to the right and crashes into a pile of wood while Jack flies off to the left and crashes through a hut. Jack picks himself up out of the rubble and grabs his dagger off the ground. As he steps out of the hole in the wall the Nightling runs right into him and breaks through the other wall. They tumble across the ground until Jack kicks the Nightling off him. They both stand up just feet from each other and walk in a circle looking at each other right in the eye. Jack grips his dagger tighter.

"Vladmir!"

The Nightling slowly falls onto all fours and watches Jack cautiously.

"Vladmir I know it is you, you can stop this."

The Nightling jumps back and lands on a rock protruding from the ground and perches itself on the edge. Its tail sways back and forth as it watches Jack.

"Don't let that creature control you! I don't want you to hurt Katz!"

The Nightling smiles as if an evil thought crossed its mind. Jack starts to get angry.

"You will not touch her!"

The Nightling lunges out at Jack and falls to the ground on top of him. Jack is now pinned to the ground with the Nightling on his chest. Above the Nightling its tail begins to glow and drip poison. Its tail strikes down just to the right of Jack's head. It tries to strike again and Jack moves out of the way. It begins to grow angry and growls at Jack and strikes again with no avail. Then a great black hand comes down and knocks the Nightling off of Jack. It throws Jack at a tree and begins to daze out. Before he falls unconscious he sees the hand pick up the Nightling and squeeze it. The Nightling struggles trying to get out of the grip and a voice comes from the darkness.

"Do not kill him. I have plans for him."

Jack falls limp and lays against the tree unconscious. The hand throws the Nightling against the ground and it screams out in pain.

"Now go and fulfill your task."

The Nightling gets up and charges through the trees. Nightmare looks down at its army and watches it diminish quickly. More and more puffs of black smoke begin to cover the battlegrounds. Nightmare spots the Nightling and watches in eagerness as it gets closer and closer to Katz. Just as the Nightling is going to strike her down with its tail an Elder from the back throws a ball of fire directly at the Nightling and sends it flying in the other direction. The Nightling screams as its skin burns and boils from the flames and runs back in Nightmare's direction. He looks back to see most if its army is gone and the men pushing the rest back behind the barrier. Nightmare fills with rage and anger like no other. It will not fail again to these witches. With one swipe of its hand all of the ragdolls vanish. Nightmare looks down to see Katz and Scott running into the forest chasing the Nightling. It smiles and waits for her to emerge from the forest. As she emerges the ground shakes and she falls down and Scott gets blown back by a forceful wind. Katz looks around to see Nightmare pulling the earth below her feet up to the sky. She looks down over the edge to see Scott looking back up at her and reaching a hand out. Sivanna comes and stands next to him and looks up to see the Nightling grab Katz's by her hair and drag her out of sight. She takes out her dagger and points it up towards Katz's direction. A small word escapes her lips.

"Helkmo."

A chill blows pass her neck and whispers into her ear.

Give her the broken sword hilt she has found for she will know what to do. Then you must summon the Luma Dragas.

Sivanna comes to and looks up to the floating rock above her. She takes Scott by the arm and takes him back to the village. She meets up with the Elders who are healing the wounded.

"Elders I have heard the words of our goddess!"

They finish tending to the wounded and come up to Sivanna.

"What did she say to you?"

"She said to save our world is to give my granddaughter the broken sword hilt she brought with her and summon Luma Dragas."

The Elders gasp and Scott runs in with the hilt of the broken sword and hands it to Sivanna.

"The goddess said she will know what to do but we need to get this to her. Nightmare has pulled a chunk of the earth to the sky with her on it. Once that moon is at its high peak he will begin that ritual."

The Elders talk amongst themselves and one leaves the gathering area. She comes back with a bag full of bottles, small pouches, chalk dust, and many other things. She hands the bag to the head Elder.

"Now we will head out and summon the Luma Dragas."

Sivanna smiles with relief and turns to Scott.

"Scott I need you to stay here and keep everything under control here."

"But I need to help Katz."

"I know you want to help her but you need to help her here."

Sivanna looks up to see to villagers carrying Jack in. Scott follows her gaze and gasps.

"Plus I believe Jack may need your help right now."

Scott nods proudly and goes to tend to Jack. The Elders and Sivanna head out to the training grounds to begin the ritual. Sivanna looks to the sky to see the moon is not far from its zenith. The moon is slowly becoming a darker and darker red as it approaches its highest point in the sky. One of the Elders takes a pouch of white chalk dust and sprinkles a circle around Sivanna. At the north, south, east, and west the Elder draws symbols in the dust. Each symbol represents night, stars, moon, or life. Then a larger circle is placed around the symbols. Sivanna paints the same symbols on herself, one on her forehead, one on each hand, and one on her chest. The Elders gather around her with staffs in hand. One begins to swing a small lantern with smoke coming from its opening; one takes a bottle and pours a drop onto the chalk. The chalk catches and lights as a burning blue fire. The Elders start to chant quietly as they bang their staffs to the ground. Sivanna looks up to the sky and raises her hands to the sky.

"Luma Dragas, Dragas ra nul-ice. Eau lumissa litna ka muvah. Ta ka itma ra ulmi sa sumuss ea, weetalay sitna eau litna mai tu."

Moon Dragon, dragon of night. Your stars light our way. In our time of need we summon you, please shine your light on us.

The circles and symbols around Sivanna brighten with every hit of the staffs. Then the lights go down and a shockwave flies across the ground in a ten foot diameter and shoot towards the sky. The light disappears in the sky. Sivanna watches the sky hoping to see something different in the dark clouds. Out of the corner of her eye she spots stars moving across the sky and then they disappear in the clouds. A gentle wind blows the chalk dust away. As she looks to the sky the stars appear once more but they seem to be closer. They get closer and closer and the Elders start to back away. A magnificent beast lands next to Sivanna. It is a dragon with a long slender body. Its body is covered in short white fur and a light silver mark goes from the top of its head down to the end of it tail. Its tail flares out into light wisps of hair that gently flow in the wind. Two long strands come from either side of its snout. Upon its head are two horns that form a beautiful crown and small round pieces orbit around it. In the center of the crown lies a dark blue stone that sparkles with the stars of the night sky. The belly of the dragon looks exactly like the night sky. It is a deep dark blue with small little white stars shining in the night. It brings it small black nose towards Sivanna and Sivanna places a hand out. They touch and the dragon's soft aquamarine eyes look into hers.

I have heard your plea and I have come to help you stop this evil that has taken over the land.

Sivanna reaches out and hugs the dragon's snout. Sivanna looks into the dragon's eyes and holds the sword hilt in front of the dragon.

"Let us takes this to my granddaughter first."

The dragon nods and kneels down to let Sivanna get on its back. Sivanna hesitates and strokes its back. She grabs hold the dragon's neck and pulls herself on its back and looks up at Nightmare.

"Let's go save the land and my granddaughter."

The dragon flies into the sky heading straight for Nightmare.

Katz pulls away from the Nightling's grip and looks around. All she could see are the dark clouds swirling around them and then a light in the sky. It is the moon but not just any moon. As it continues to rise into the night sky its white luminous color slowly darkens into a deep red. With fear in her eyes, she looks up to see Nightmare grinning down at her. Katz tries to run but stops at the edge of the rock. She stares down into the endless cloud abyss as the small rocks that fell disappear. She slowly backs away from the edge.

"There is nowhere to run. Mwhahahahahaha."

Katz turns around to see the Nightling standing before her and falls to the ground.

"What are you going to do to me?"

Nightmare just chuckles.

"Only time will tell. Once the moon has reached its position in the sky…"

The Nightling takes Katz by the wrist and drags her closer to Nightmare. As they get closer the earth breaks forming large chunks of rock that gather forming an altar underneath the moon. Katz tries to pull free and the Nightling's grip only gets tighter.

" LET ME GO!"

The Nightling turns around and shrieks in her face and leaves her speechless. Katz continues to pull away as they get closer to the altar. Nightmare waits patiently, anticipating the opportune time. Katz takes hold of her necklace and prays to the moon goddess for help. A small breeze blows past her and gently whispers in her ear.

Sing.

Katz pauses and is stunned by a voice coming from the wind. Then it clicked. The song she learned from her grandmother, a song to sing when feeling afraid; the song that somehow affected Nightmare before. She looks up towards Nightmare and starts to sing. The song came from deep within filling her with hope and strength. The Nightling grips tighter as it screams out in pain. Nightmare glares down in disgust and lifts its dark hand and swings it in Katz's direction. Katz closes her eyes waiting for the hit to come. She feels a cold breeze and doesn't open her eyes for she knows she is falling. Thoughts race through her head, emotions bringing tears to her eyes. This is it. This is how it ends. The world to fall in darkness as Nightmare strikes her down with the Blood Moon high in the sky ending all light as they know it.

Chapter 18

In the mist of her dark abyss a soft angel-like touch is felt upon her arm. She feels like she is being lifted up high. She opens her eyes looking to see the heavenly embrace of the goddess bringing her in from the dark. As her eyes open she feels a face against hers. Katz looks towards the face to see her grandmother holding her tight. Sivanna looks into Katz eyes with upmost happiness.

"The goddess will not take you, not yet."

Katz embraces Sivanna and hears a voice in her head.

Child of the Goddess I am happy you are safe. Now we must complete that which has been foretold.

Sivanna holds out a broken sword hilt to Katz. She gives her one last hug, kisses her on the cheek, and falls. Katz reaches for her even though she is now far from her grasp. Sivanna lands on the levitating rock, and pulls out her dagger; before her stands the Nightling, watching her with its red eyes. She takes a fighting stance.

"This is for my daughter."

Katz watches on as Sivanna and the Nightling battle to the death. She looks back up at Nightmare just in time to avoid his attack. The Luma Dragas speaks to her.

Child we must end this monster's destruction. Are you ready?

Katz looks down at the broken sword hilt then to Sivanna.

"Yes, but we must go do something first."

They go deep into the forest and weaved in and about the trunks of the trees. They came upon a clearing just in front of a moss covered cave. Katz jumps off the dragon and heads towards the cave and enters. The villagers gasp as she enters and walks up to the Elders.

"Elders, I ask of those who can still fight to help me in this final battle against Nightmare. Will you help?"

The Elders talk amongst themselves and nod in agreement. The men bore their armor once more and take hold of their weapons. Katz went over to Jack and Scott. She holds out her hand in front of them.

"Want to join me?"

The boys smiled and placed their hands upon hers. All who were going out to battle form a small group in front of the Elders. The Elders hold their staffs above the crowd.

"May the goddess protect you and guide you on your way to victory!"

Then the group left the cave. The men say goodbye to their wives, lovers, and children as they exit the cave. Jack and Scott follow behind Katz and came upon a great dragon. Katz takes the dragon gently by the snout and caresses it.

Will you be able to carry us three to the battle?

Yes, and I will help in any way I can.

Katz takes the gem from her necklace and places it into the hilt of the sword. The simple hilt once again became the sword of light. She takes hold of the sword and jumps on the back of the dragon along with Jack and Scott. She raises the sword into the air.

"NOW ONTO NIGHTMARE AND BRING PEACE ONCE MORE!"

The crowd cheers and charges into the forest, and Scott, Jack, and Katz fly to the sky to face the darkness before them and to stop it once and for all.

Sivanna begins to feel weary from her fight. The Nightling has thrashed her left and right leaving her bruised and tired. Sivanna stands for what may be her last but at least she knows her granddaughter is alright. She holds up her dagger and waits for the attack. The Nightling crawls on all fours and vanishes. Sivanna looks about her to see where in the darkness the creature may appear. Then from behind a low growl and she turns to see the Nightling and something else. Katz has jumped from the dragon and kicked the Nightling away. Now Katz, Jack, and Scott stand before Sivanna. Sivanna just smiles.

"You look so much like your mother."

Then they hear chants and cheers from the forest below. When they look down they see surge after surge of people come from the forest, weapons in hand. Nightmare raises his hands into the air and brings the ragdolls back once more to fight the villagers. So, down below the villagers fight, and up on the rock Jack, Scott, Sivanna, and Katz fight with the demon itself. Katz hugs Sivanna and looks up to her.

"Now I must go. Scott, Jack, help my grandmother keep that Nightling distracted."

The boys nod and take their attention to the Nightling getting up from the hit. Katz jumps back on the dragon with her sword of light in hand. She nods to her grandmother and flies off towards Nightmare. Sivanna, Jack, and Scott take on the dreaded Nightling, the villagers take on the ragdolls, and Katz takes on the demon of darkness.

As Katz gets closer Nightmare's rage grows as a dark mist envelopes them. Katz looks around to see nothing but herself, the dragon, and Nightmare. She holds her sword up high and charges it. She yells out into the darkness and strikes Nightmare. She turns to see it has not affected it. Katz charges once more but this time a black twister strikes down in her path and sends her back. Then it lashes out with a mighty black hand just missing Katz but hits the dragon square on. A large gash lies open on the dragon's side as silver blood oozes from the wound. Katz strokes the back of the dragon's neck.

Are you alright?

I may have a wound but I can still help you stop Nightmare.

But, I don't know how to stop him.

Then let us call upon the goddess herself, repeat after me.

Okay.

Oh great goddess, the bringer of light in darkness.

Oh great goddess, the bringer of light in darkness.

Though we have great strength.

Though we have great strength.

Give us the knowledge to stop Nightmare!

Give us the knowledge to stop Nightmare!

As they wait for the answer from the goddess Nightmare sends a creature out. From afar Katz does not recognize it. As it comes closer she freezes in fear, a great black beast with enormous wings and a red eyed rider upon its back. The rider holds a sword of burning red fire-like light in its right hand. It makes a head on attack at Katz. Katz moves off to the side and strikes the beast down its bulky side. The creature screams an ear-splitting scream as thick black liquid came from its side. The rider lifts its sword and it grows into a long flaming rope. It whips it out towards Katz and wraps it around the dragon's neck and pulls it towards itself. The dragon roars in pain and Katz panics as she is pulled closer to the rider and its hideous beast. Then a gentle breeze wraps around and a voice whispers in her ear. At that moment it seems that time has stopped to let her hear this message.

The Sword of Light will penetrate Nightmare but only you can stop it from the inside. There you will find the object that will weaken him. Hold your sword toward Nightmare, leap from the dragon, and call out Guahlitna.

Then time begins once more and Katz pulls the dragon out of the rider's grip. As the rider gets ready for another attack Katz leaps from the dragons back and points her sword's tip to Nightmare.

"GUAHLITNA!!!"

A ball of light forms at the tip of the sword and the outer blades begin to spin and form a barrier around Katz. Then with great force the blade pulls Katz towards Nightmare. The rider tries to stop her but breaks into pieces as she flies right through the rider and its beast. Sivanna looks up to see a comet of light fly across the sky and straight into Nightmare's chest. The swirling clouds died down and great chains of light take hold of Nightmare's hands and hold them away from its body. Nightmare struggles to get free with no avail.

Nightmare sends spell after spell trying to break the chains. Its fury grows and enraged clouds electrify the sky with purple-white lightning and heavy rains pour down on the battle below. Sivanna looks on to see if Katz will escape from within Nightmare, for there she must face her greatest fear of all.

Katz looks about the endless dark abyss that surrounds her. The only light she has is the sword she wields in her hands. A faint pulsing sound comes from her right. She turns to see an orb that glows with a blackish purple hue and pulsates like the beating of a heart. Katz now knows this is what will weaken and stop Nightmare. She begins kicking her feet in the space she floats as if she was normal running outside. She begins to move towards the orb and as it gets in her grasp it begins to move away. The closer she got the quicker and farther the orb went. Now a great distance stands between Katz and the orb. Again she feels the breeze around her but this time very faint and very quietly in her ear she could only make out two words.

.....be..brave.

Katz looks out to the orb and begins to fall. She feels a cold wetness around her. She could feel the air trying to escape from her lungs and she sinks deeper and deeper into the water-like liquid. She begins to panic and flail her arms trying to reach the surface and the faster she moved the faster she sinks. Her heart pounds in her chest as she begins to lose all hope. Then whispers spin around her.

Give up.

You'll never make it.

Say good bye.

You are not strong enough.

Fall forever.

Katz looks up to see the orb getting farther and farther from her reach. The feeling of failure and hopelessness begin to fall in and her heart sinks into its cold depths. Katz closes her eyes ready to let go of her last breath. Then a familiar voice echoes in the darkness.

Katz.

She looks up to see no one and then she hears it again.

Katz.

She now knows it is coming from the orb.

Do you trust me?

Her eyes fill with tears as that voice warms her heart. She reaches out with one hand and begins to swim. She can see the orb coming closer and closer within her reach. The horrid beast flew by trying to scare her and make her give up once more, but the words echo in her head filling her with more and more strength. A dark beast came head on and she struck it down with a swing of her sword. Finally the orb hovers before her. She reaches out and takes the orb in her hand, then images of her friends and family flash before her, each of them falling to their deaths. She reaches out for them but cannot grab their hands. She watches one by one has they reach the bottom and no longer move. Their screams of terror ring around her.

Katz why?

Why didn't you save us?

I am your friend?

I love you!

Don't let me fall!

She frantically watches around as her friends fall over and over again to their demise. She falls to her knees and cries for the images to stop. A dark voice speaks out.

If you wish this to stop then drop the orb and no harm will become of them.

"You won't harm them, not one of them?"

Yes.

Katz looks at the orb in her hands and her falling friends around her. She slowly uncurls her fingers and the ball slowly rolls towards her fingertips. She closes her eyes in defeat. Then gentle hands take hold of her hands and stop the orb from rolling. She looks up to see no one but feels a comforting presence.

Don't let go. Your friends are counting on you.

"But they said if I let go of the orb they won't harm them."

A silence hangs between her and the voice.

So thought I.

Katz heart sinks as she feels that sadness from the presence before her. She looks at the orb before her and focuses on it. She wipes the tears from her face and takes hold of the orb in one hand and points the sword straight in front of her with the other. She ignores her friends cry for help and the water creeping up her body. She stares straight down into the abyss.

"GUAHLITNA!!!"

Once again a ball of light forms at the tip of the sword, the outer blades spin, and she flies through the abyss with the orb in hand.

Sivanna hears a blood curdling scream from below. She looks over the edge to see the ragdolls writhing in pain. As each one screams out they burst into a cloud of black smoke and disappear. The villagers watch as their enemies numbers dwindled. Then Sivanna hears a horrid shriek behind her. The Nightling, still having the will to fight, screams out in pain. Sivanna looks up to Nightmare, who is now free from his chains, but hunched over in pain. It twists its hands into tight fists and lifts it head just a bit to let everyone see a small blue light glow from the center of its chest. As Nightmare throws its head back a comet of light bursts from its chest, it hovers above the floating rock and bursts into sparkling dots of light. Katz now stands before Sivanna with the orb in hand. Katz walks up to Sivanna.

"What do I do with the orb now?"

The rock they stand upon shakes knocking them to the ground. They look up to see a figure that is not quite solid and not quite mist. It slowly gets up showing enraged red eyes and a set of angry sharp teeth. It starts to walk slowly towards them.

"You will not win.....will not."

Sivanna takes Katz by the shoulders.

"You must destroy the orb."

Sivanna takes the dagger from her side and gives it to Katz.

"Use this to destroy the orb. It is the only thing that is holding Nightmare here."

Katz looks over to see Nightmare still trying to make its way towards them. It tries reaching out with its hands but they neither stretch long enough to reach the orb nor Katz. Katz kneels on the ground and places the orb between her knees. She holds the dagger above her head and looks up to see that the Nightling is coming straight for her. She strikes down on the orb. Bright flashes of purple lights emanate from the orb and black ooze leaks from the cracked surface. The light of the orb pulsates slower. As Nightmare falls and the Nightling falls before her screaming but its voice changed and sounding very familiar. Before Katz completely pushes that dagger through she kneels down next to the Nightling who is now gripping at its chest. The Nightling begins to change. Its dark skin becoming torn clothing, its claws into fingers, its horns into ears, its pupils returned to its eyes, and white hair grew upon its head. Katz eyes fills with tears as she now is looking down at Vladmir. With his eyes closed he grips his chest where crimson blood came leaking through. Katz takes hold of Vladmir's head in her lap as tears fall from her face.

"Vladmir, I didn't know it was you."

Vladmir gasps for air as the pain shoots through his body.

"It is not your fault...but..you need to finish...what you started."

Katz looks over at the orb with the dagger sticking straight out of the top. She could see its pulsating light getting slower and slower. She pulls it towards her. Then a horrible thought finally clicked.

"This is your heart?"

"Katz, you...must...finish..."

Katz takes hold of Vladmir's hand and shakes her head.

"No, I can't."

"This will be the only way to stop Nightmare."

Katz looks up to see Nightmare is still trying to get to them in his weakened state. Vladmir takes his other hand and gently strokes her face. Katz rubs her cheek against his cold hand. While he has her distracted he takes her other hand and pushed the dagger through the orb shattering it into pieces. Katz pulls her hand away in terror and looks down at Vladmir. She watches as his last breath escapes and his hand falls from her face. Tear after tear falls from her face as she lays her head on Vladmir's lifeless body. She just couldn't believe it.

"VLADMIR! VLADMIR!? Please Vladmir come back..."

She looks down to see him but no words came from his quiet mouth. Katz cries uncontrollably. Jack and Scott came over to comfort Katz. Sivanna watches as Nightmare slowly falls apart and melts away in the darkness. Even as it falls it continues its last path. Before the evil being finally vanishes it said one last thing.

"Darkness never dies for it lives in all of you. Mwahahahahahah."

Its laughter fades away as the last of Nightmare falls back into the darkness seeping back into the earth. Sivanna walks over to Katz who is still at Vladmir's side, her head lying down on his chest as she strokes his cold cheek. In between quieting sobs she said three last words to him.

"I.....love...you.."

Sivanna helps Katz up as the rock they stand upon slowly lowers back down to the earth. As the rock settles back into its place the villagers look upon the sad sight before them. Even though the evil has been vanquished darkness still covers the land for many lives have been taken in this battle. Jack takes Katz from Sivanna. Scott walks with Jack and Katz back to the village. Sivanna gets some of the men to build a stretcher to take Vladmir's body back with them for a proper good bye.

As to those who fought the great battle came back to tell the war had finally ended, many of those waiting cried for their lost husbands and fathers. Vladmir's body is covered and taken to the Elders hut so Katz will not see. Jack and Scott take Katz back to Sivanna's hut and sat with her on the bed to help her cope with Vladmir's passing. Katz hides her face in Jack's shoulder and Scott holds her hand.

"Katz it will be alright. Time will heal all wounds."

"No it won't."

Jack gives her a hug.

"Yes it will. Me, Scott, and your grandma will be there to help you along the way."

"But I loved him."

Katz begins to cry once more and Jack hugs her trying to comfort her knowing deep down that is all a friend could do. Finally Katz falls asleep and the boys cover her with a blanket and let her rest. Jack and Scott head out to help the others with preparations and cleaning up the debris lying around. They look around to see that the sun is finally shining when the great sun bird was released as Nightmare was vanquished. Yet even with the sun in the sky low clouds of sadness hang over the village. Scott helped with food preparations while Jack helped clean up the remnants of war. Sivanna is with the Elders all day discussing what needs to be done for the day and the days after. As dusk approaches Sivanna looks to the sky to see the Luma Dragas cross the sky bringing a blanket of shining stars and a beautiful white moon behind it. Sivanna is tired from the day's talks and tasks and heads home to her hut to rest for tomorrow for it too will be filled with many more tasks to do. When she enters her hut she sees Katz has pulled the blanket up and over her head. Sivanna just chuckles and pulls the blanket down.

Sivanna backs away from the blanket and pillows and gasps. Katz is gone.

Chapter 19

Sivanna looks about the room and runs back out of the hut. She panics and looks in every direction trying to see if Katz is anywhere. She cups her hands over her mouth.

"KATZ!! KATZ WHERE ARE YOU! KAAATZ!"

Jack sits up from his bed and rubs his eyes and listens to the noise that has awakened him. He stands up and heads over to the window. As he peers through the window, he sees Sivanna frantically running around the village calling out for someone. Jack puts his ear to the window and his eyes widen. Sivanna is looking for Katz! She is calling for her! What happened to Katz? Jack turns to Scott and shakes him.

"SCOTT! SCOTT, KATZ IS MISSING! GET UP!"

Scott turns over and moans and quietly goes back to sleep. Jack runs over to his bed and takes the pillow and smacks Scott in the head with it. Scott jumps up and puts his hand up in a defensive position as he looks to see what hit him.

"Scott, Katz is missing. Sivanna is out there looking for her."

"Then why didn't you say so?"

Scott quickly gets up, changes back into his pants, and Jack just shakes his head.

"I did sleeping beauty just didn't want to listen."

Scott looks over with a guilty smile. They both run out of the hut and meet Sivanna in the middle of the village. Sivanna continues to yell out into the night and small lights inside of each of the huts flicker to life. Villagers slowly come from their huts to see what is going on, Sivanna paces back and forth looking in every direction. Scott yawns as Jack approaches Sivanna.

"What is going on?"

Sivanna looks straight at him with tears of fright and worry in her eyes.

"I..I..I don't know. I went back to the hut and she wasn't there. I..."

A thought pops into her mind and she charges into the village with Scott and Jack close behind. They dodge villagers and jump over piles of debris. Scott catches himself as he trips over some broken wood.

"Sivanna where are you going?"

Sivanna stops in front of the Elders' hut. Jack and Scott come up from behind, panting from the run. Jack looks up to see Sivanna gently push the curtain aside from the doorway as if she is afraid to go inside. The boys follow behind and enter the hut. When they enter they find Vladmir lying upon the makeshift cot with a soft white blanket pulled up to his chin. Kneeling down beside the body is Katz with a small blanket wrapped around her shoulders. She has her head lying against the side of the cot with her hand on the blanket over Vladmir's hand. She gently strokes the blanket as she quietly looks up to Vladmir's face. A small tear glistens in the faint candle light that sits quietly next to her and with her other hand she holds her necklace close to her. Sivanna, Scott, nor Jack knows how to approach her. They hesitate and Sivanna steps forward.

"Katz, I was worried about you."

Katz didn't respond. Scott fidgets with his hands.

"Katz?"

Katz lowers her head and sighs and continues to stroke Vladmir's hand. Jack clears his throat.

"Katz, he is gone. I, uh, mean we can help you get through this."

Katz lets out a small chuckle.

"You may think so but I feel like he is still here."

The faint glow of the moon looks down upon the group as it peers through the skylight in the ceiling of the hut. It watches as the young girl mourns for her loved one. A small breeze blows through the opening and swirls about the room. Katz pulls the blanket tighter around her arms, standing just below the opening in the ceiling stand two figures. One is Vladmir looking gloomily over at his lifeless self and Katz crying beside him. Even though he no longer lives he feels like his heart is torn to pieces. Beside him stands a goddess of a figure. Her pale blue dress gently flows about her. A soft woven silk lays flowing over her dress around her hips and sparkles in the moon's light. Her top is held up by one strap across her left shoulder. Small silver stones twinkle across her top and a long silver, see-through piece of cloth falls gently from her left shoulder wrapping around her body. Her wrists are adorned with shining silver rings and sing the song of the night. A necklace made of beautiful blue-green moonstones hangs from her neck. The very center stone is a small version of the full moon showing, then following it are the different phases of the moon. She has a gentle and caring face with soft white eyes. Her long black hair falls upon her pale white shoulders. Around her waist two belts of stars and galaxies orbit around her both tilting on opposite angles crossing just above her hips. Upon her head the most beautiful crown sits. Lines of silver intertwine with one another forming a crown and they always seem to be flowing with life. At the end of each line, as light flows within, small twinkling stars appears. In the center of the crown lies a beautiful round moonstone that shines a beautiful sapphire blue in the light. She looks upon Vladmir as he watches Katz.

"I wish I could speak to her and tell her I am alright."

"They cannot see nor hear you."

"I know. I just wish there were some way."

Vladmir looks back up to see Sivanna trying to take Katz out of the hut. Katz continues to refuse and her friends hesitate to help Sivanna. Jack and Scott try talking Katz into leaving but nothing works. Sivanna struggles to keep a hold on Katz but she breaks free. She turns and walks back to Vladmir's body. She kneels before him and she looks up to the ceiling as seeing right through it. She takes hold of her necklace and holds her arm with the other.

"Luma Guah, my guardian, please bring Vladmir back. I don't care what the cost. I just…"

Katz looks back down at Vladmir's body and smiles. Vladmir watches curiously and Luma Guah listens quietly.

"I just want him to be with me. I felt safe with him. When I was in Nightmare, it was his voice I heard that saved me. He pulled me from my darkness. I trust you Vladmir, I trust you."

Vladmir just stands in awe and sighs.

"She did hear me."

Luma Guah smiles at the love that these two beings shared, a bond so strong that death can't even separate them. Katz falls back onto to her heels and begins to cry quietly. Luma Guah glides slowly across to Katz and spins once around her. Katz lifts her head up and stares off into the distance. The goddess leans over and whispers into Katz's ear. Vladmir waits in silent anticipation.

Child of mine you have listened and you have been heard.

Luma Guah stands back up and comes back to Vladmir. She leans over and kisses Vladmir on the lips. Their eyes meet.

"Never let anything break your bond."

Vladmir let out a long sigh and grips his chest as a sudden throb of pain wracks him. He grips tighter as a second throb hits his chest. He looks up to the goddess to see the night sky behind her. She smiles and Vladmir falls. Vladmir looks down to see millions of stars pass him and feel the wind rushing past. The stars fade away and Vladmir closes his eyes and continues through the black abyss listening to the faint beating of a heart.

Katz sits upon her heels and just cries silently to herself. Then a soft sound echoes about the room. She looks up to see that Sivanna, Jack, and Scott have noticed as well. The sound grows louder and they all recognize it as a sound of a beating heart. Katz quickly stands and breathes in anticipation as she watches for any movement. She looks up and down Vladmir's body waiting for any sign. Then as quiet as the night the blanket begins to rise gently up and down into the air. Katz walks over and lays her ear upon Vladmir's chest. Tears of joy fall from her face as the sound of air entering and escaping the lungs pass by and the beating of a living heart. Katz feels a hand slowly come up at the back of her head and she looks up at Vladmir's face. The happiest smile fills Katz's face as she looks back into Vladmir's eyes. Vladmir chuckles.

"I missed you."

Katz gasps and takes hold of Vladmir around his neck and doesn't let go.

"I missed you, too."

They look into each other's eyes and a sudden tiredness falls upon them. Vladmir's eyes close and Katz falls to the floor with her eyes closed as well. Sivanna and Scott run to the both of them. Jack stands at the doorway not knowing what to do. Sivanna signals to Scott to help lift Katz to a nearby cot. Scott covers Katz with a blanket as Sivanna runs out the door to go find the Elders.

Sivanna and the Elders stay up all night trying to wake Katz and Vladmir from this deep slumber. Jack and Scott wait outside the hut hoping for any news. Scott is playing with some small stones and sticks on the ground while Jack paces back and forth. Every now and then Jack would look up at the hut to see if anyone is coming out. Scott looks up at Jack.

"Dude, you need to relax. Everything will be fine."

"How would you know? Anything could be going on in there!"

"Yes but you don't know if it is anything bad."

Jack grunts and falls to the ground on his butt and watches the door with his arms crossed. Scott just shrugs his shoulders and shakes his head. Then Sivanna and the Elders exit from the hut. Two of the guards that were with them block the doorway, Jack jumps up and goes up to the Elders. All the Elders looked ravaged and exhausted. A couple of the villagers went and helped the eldest Elders to their huts. Sivanna walks over to a nearby tree and falls against it to the ground. She looks up to the sky and just sighs. Jack and Scott run over to Sivanna who looks up with swollen eyes. She must have been crying all night. Scott kneels down and places a hand on her shoulder. Jack kneels down on one knee and looks to Sivanna for any news. Sivanna closes her eyes and just shakes her head. Jack stands back up frustrated with the situation. Scott takes a seat next to Sivanna and tries to comfort her.

"I and the Elders have tried everything. Spells upon spells, potion after potion and nothing seems to have any affect. We have made no progress."

Sivanna hides her face in her knees and begins to cry quietly. Scott takes Sivanna gently by the hand.

"We will find a way. There is always a way."

Jack throws his hands into the air with anger.

"Then what is the way Scott? They have tried everything! What could be left to do! WHAT IS THE SOLUTION?"

Scott stands up and looks seriously at Jack.

"Jack you need to calm down. We will find the answer."

Jack pushes Scott into the tree and holds him up against it. He looks into his eyes.

"What happens if we don't find one?"

Jack turns and walks away leaving Scott rubbing the soreness from his arms. Suki comes up to see Sivanna and is pushed aside by Jack as he walks by. Suki watches as Jack leaves from view feeling the anger as he passed. She turns and finds Sivanna and Scott by the tree. Suki kneels down in front of them.

"The Elders believe in pray."

Sivanna and Scott look confusingly up at Suki.

"Want us to pray. Elders believe Luma Guah is last chance."

Sivanna nods and stands up and dusts off her knees.

"Alright, tonight we will gather around the fire pit and pray to the goddess for Katz and Vladmir's safety and to bring them back to us. For now I must rest. Go and tell the others and I will meet you then."

Suki and Scott nod and head out to tell the fellow villagers of the news. Sivanna walks into her hut and sits upon her bed. She slides off her shoes and pulls the blanket to her shoulders and closes her eyes. Before she falls into a deep sleep she prays to the goddess.

"Luma Guah, where ever they are please.....bring them back....please..."

Then Sivanna quickly drifts off to sleep.

Night draws near as everyone begins to gather at the fire pit. Four men bring out Vladmir's and Katz's bodies and lay them side by side in front of the fire pit. Sivanna looks down to see Katz's lifeless face glow faintly in the fire's light. She kneels down and gently brushes her cheek and then joins the Elders who are waiting for everyone to arrive. Xolstice leads Suki, Scott, and Jack to the front where the Elders are sitting. They sit down facing out to the crowd of people waiting patiently for the praying to begin. The head Elder walks in front of Scott and Jack and held out her hands. In her hands are two rings with the same stone that hung from her neck. The boys reach out and take the rings out of her hand.

"We need everyone to help bring back Vladmir and Katz. We usually do a ceremony to bring new people to our village but we can't due to certain matters. Welcome to Azmala's family."

The Elder walks away as Scott slides the ring on his finger. Jack looks at the ring. Both his and Scott's are the same with a simple silver band with a single blue stone set in the ring. Jack turns the ring in his finger and as he watches the stone shimmers with a blue shine. He slides the ring on his smallest finger. Most of the Elders sit upon the ground and only the head Elder stands. She lifts her hands and her staff into the air. The villages take one another's hand and join as one. Suki and Xolstice join hands. Suki reaches for Scott's hand and takes hold. Scott looks down and smiles and turns and takes Jack's. Jack nods. The villagers begin to mumble under their breath with words that neither Jack nor Scott could hear. Scott looks over to Suki.

"Say *Luma Guah*."

"Luma Guah?"

"Yes, call upon her."

Suki turns her head and continues to follow the villagers in their chant. Scott and Jack join them. Their chant becomes louder and every stone that each villager held begins to glow brightly. Jack looks up to the Elders to see the head Elder calling out in the ancient language. Her fellow Elders hover just a little above the ground and the symbols on their cheeks begin to illuminate. Their eyes spring open to reveal brightly glowing white eyes. The wind begins to pick up blowing leaves around. As Jack looks around the glowing light shoots from underneath him. He watches as the light fingers out like lightening across the ground. It slithers up trunks of trees and the dim light coming from each and every leaf grows brighter. Then the fire before them blows and flies to the sky in a great ball. As the fire gathers into an orb shape the color of the fire from the pit to the sky goes from reds and oranges to a shimmering bright white. The flames course and pulse from within the orb. The flames begin to pull away and twist. The head Elder begins to pound her stick on the ground and even brighter light shoots across the ground with each hit. A great rumble echoes across the land. Everyone looks up to see a great dragon made of coursing white fire. It lowers it head to the head Elder. The chanting stops and the head Elder looks up to the dragon. A small silence lingers in the air and then she calls out.

" Great Dragon of the White Flame! We pray to you to take our message to our great goddess, Luma Guah. Please bring back the ones we lost to an endless slumber. Their hearts beat but no words are ever spoken. We ask of the goddess to hear our plea!"

Their eyes lock and a silence lingers. A low grumble comes from the dragon as it begins to speak.

"Your prayer has been heard and now I will take it to our goddess."

The dragon backs away from her and dives into the red flames and disappears. Then it fires straight to the night sky with a mighty roar. The villagers watch on until they can no longer see the dragon. Then the night goes silent and dark for the fire has been extinguished. Scott looks around and sees everyone getting up. He turns his head to Suki who is also getting up.

"Wait, shouldn't we sit and wait for what happens?"

Suki pulls Scott up from the ground and smiles.

"We do nothing. Up to the goddess now."

Jack looks over with confusion and anger.

"So we just sat there for nothing? Nothing happened!"

Sivanna steps down from the other Elders and stands before Jack.

"We cannot do anything else for now. Our prayer has been sent and is now up to the goddess to decide."

"No! What happens if she decides not to wake them up? What do we do then?"

Sivanna looks at him with sad eyes.

"Then they both will lie together in an endless slumber never to wake again...."

"NO!"

Jack storms away as the rest watch him disappear into the crowd. Scott looks up to Sivanna.

"As I was trying to say, they may never awake but they just might wake one day."

Sivanna looks over at the bodies as they are carried back into the Elder's hut. She looks up to the night sky and watches the stars twinkle and shine waiting for an answer.

Chapter 20

Katz and Vladmir stand together holding each other in their arms. They stand in place that looks like the night sky but the trees and the grass around them are made from the stars and shades of pinks, blues, and purples fill in the gaps between them. They look into each other's eyes. Vladmir gently rubs the side of Katz's face to wipe away the tears.

"Vladmir, I thought I was going to lose you."

"I would never leave you, never."

Katz giggles and Vladmir just chuckles. Luma Guah appears next to them and standing beside her is a dragon made of white flame. She bows to the dragon as it bows its head. She turns to Katz and Vladmir as the dragon shoots to the sky and becomes a bright glowing star. Luma Guah smiles at the love they share. She holds out a gray stone with a white light pulsating across its surface. Vladmir and Katz look up to her.

"Your curse is not fully removed. With the touch of this stone, the darkness that still lingers in you will be gone. The curse will be gone."

Vladmir's ears perked up.

"That means everything will go back to the way they were."

"Not exactly."

Katz looks with worry.

"What do you mean?"

"The darkness is inside you both. Katz you will be fine but Vladmir will be fine too with some small changes. The darkness inside of him was great and it changed him. Vladmir, the only way to rid the last bit of is to give you a gift."

"A gift?"

"Yes a gift from me will rid you of the darkness."

"So what is this gift?"

"That is for you to discover on your own."

Vladmir looks questioningly at the stone. Then Katz places her hand on the stone and looks up to Vladmir.

"It will be okay."

Vladmir reaches out with his hand and as he touches the stone he kisses Katz on the lips. Katz is caught off guard but her heart begins to flutter with love. A bright light consumes them. The light fades and both Vladmir and Katz lie on the ground holding hands. Luma Guah takes the stone and throws it to the darkest part of the sky. She looks back down and smiles.

"They are waiting for you."

As she wipes her hand across the sky the stars shower down on Katz and Vladmir as they fall down into the darkness lighting their way home.

Scott is awakened by a bright light and thought it was the morning sun. He gets out of bed and opens the door. He looks up to see the night sky and not a sunrise. He runs back in and starts shaking Jack in his bed.

"JACK! JACK! WAKE UP! I SAW A BRIGHT LIGHT BUT IT WASN'T THE SUN! THE STARS ARE STILL SHINING! JAAAACK!"

Jack rolls over with tired red eyes and glares at Scott.

"You probably had a dream now go back to bed."

Jack rolls over and goes back to sleep. Scott looks about the room frantically and then a thought comes to his mind. He sighs and closes his eyes.

"I'm going to regret this."

He grabs an object from his bag and tip-toes quietly over to Jack. He presses down the button and the loudest horn blast came from the tiny cone. He drops the horn as Jack stands before him puffing out with anger. Scott curls down and darts for the door.

"SCOOOOOTTTTTTT!!!!"

Scott runs out the door as fast as he could, praying that Jack won't kill him. He notices the light and runs towards it. Then something runs right into his back pile-driving him into the ground. He turns over to see a very angry Jack panting in front of him.

"Give me a good reason not to plow you into the ground right now!"

Scott looks out of the corner of his eye.

"There is the light I was telling you about."

Jack looks over and covers his face with his hand for the light nearly blinded his tired eyes. Scott slowly crawls out of Jack's grip and stands up.

"Come on, we need to follow it."

Jack and Scott run into the village to try and find where this light is coming from. As they get closer they realize the light is coming from the Elder's hut. So, they take a sharp turn back and run to Sivanna's hut. Scott runs in and gently tries to wake Sivanna up. Jack rubs his eyes.

"Why didn't you wake me up like that?"

"I did, you said I was dreaming."

Jack grunts and rubs his face. Scott shakes Sivanna gently until she quietly groans.

"Sivanna, you need to wake up. Something is up in the Elder's hut."

Sivanna gets up slowly and rubs her eye and yawns.

"What did you say Scott?"

"There is a light coming from the Elder's hut!"

Sivanna stands and runs quickly out of the hut towards the Elder's hut. She stands in front of the hut panting and out of breath. She covers her eyes with her arm trying to look into the door of the hut but the light is too bright.

"Boys go to the other huts and wake Xolstice, Suki, and the others."

They boys run off and Sivanna stands before the door. Within a few minutes almost every villager is standing outside the Elder's hut. Xolstice comes running up to Sivanna in her long pale pink and blue gown.

"Sivanna what is going on?"

"I don't know the boys came and woke me up."

Scott came up and fell on the ground before her and just gasps for air.

"I....told her...that a bright..ahem..light woke me."

One of the Elder's came up to Sivanna.

"I see a bright light has woken up the village?"

"Yes....."

The light suddenly extinguishes. Silence and darkness surround the villagers as they wait for something to exit the hut.

Anna wakes up and rubs her head and looks over at Vladmir who too is rubbing his head. She chuckles as Vladmir sits up. They give each other a hug and look into each other's eyes.

"Ah Vladmir, your eyes are blue again."

"Yeah, but my hair is still white though."

Anna brushes her hand through his hair.

"I think it looks nice on you."

"I thought that monster killed you."

"No Nightmare said it was to make sure the bond was final between you and it."

"So what happened to you? Why didn't you come back?"

"I....."

They both look over to see Sivanna standing in the doorway. Sivanna's heart leaps for joy. She runs over and falls to her knees and hugs Anna. Jack and Scott enter the door followed by Suki, Xolstice, and the Elders. Sivanna just breaks down into tears of happiness. She holds Anna tighter.

"I missed you so much Anna. I thought you were gone."

"The goddess let us come back."

Sivanna hugs Anna again. Vladmir sits back and smiles. Sivanna reaches out with a hand and pulls

Vladmir into the hug. They stand up and head towards the door. Jack, Scott, Suki, Xolstice, and the Elder head out first before Sivanna, Anna, and Vladmir exit the hut. As Anna and Vladmir exit the hut the villagers cry in an uproar and cheer. The great goddess, Luma Guah, let them awaken from their endless slumber.

The next day is the feast day of Anna and Vladmir's return. Food is prepared, decorations put up, and much more is done. Everyone did everything they could to make this day special. Anna, Vladmir, Sivanna, Scott, and Jack sit with one another around a table talking up a storm.

"So your real name is Anna?"

"Yes, Katz was given to me to protect me from Nightmare."

Sivanna smiles.

"When she came wandering from the forest in terror I came up to her. She didn't remember who she was. I was lucky that day Nightmare didn't realize that she is from the bloodline of the moon goddess. So to protect her I gave her the name Katz and brought her to your world."

Scott smiles.

"And there is where we became friends."

They all laughed at Scott's remark. Anna snuggles up to Vladmir.

"That was something I didn't know. I thought I lost her forever. The only things I had to remember her by were memories, the garden, and the rose. That's how Nightmare had a hold on me."

"But we broke it."

Vladmir takes her by the chin and Anna rubs her nose against his and giggles. Sivanna takes a small box from under the table.

"This was also with you when you came out of the forest. I kept it safe."

Anna takes the box and opens it. It is the moon ring that Vladmir had given her on the night of the party and that terrible event. She takes it from the box smiling with glee and puts it on.

"I thought I lost the ring when I noticed it wasn't on my finger when I woke up yesterday. Thank you."

The crew chatted the day away. When it came time for the festivities, Vladmir is sent out to help with the final decorations so Anna can get ready for the night.

Sivanna helps get Anna's dress on from the day she first came back to the village. Scott went to the kitchen to help set the food for the party. Jack stays with Sivanna and Anna. Sivanna gets up and leaves to get some more thread to fix Anna's dress. Once Sivanna left Jack came over and sat next to Anna.

"Hey..uh..Katz..uh.. I mean Anna."

"Yes."

Jack twiddles with his thumbs and becomes nervous. Anna waits curiously to what Jack will say. Jack sighs.

"I am glad that you are back. I wish you and Vladmir the best of luck."

Anna watches quizzically as Jack walks to the door.

"I am glad we are friends."

Then Jack leaves the hut leaving Anna alone and puzzled by their conversation. Sivanna pops her head into the door.

"Is everything alright? Jack seemed gloomy."

"Yeah."

Sivanna takes the needle and thread and finishes the last touches to the dress.

"There now you are ready for the party."

The festivities are a blast. A few of the villagers got together and made a band and played music all night long. People laugh, dance, and sing the night away. When it is time to eat, lines and lines of people brought out plate after plate of food to the tables. As they sit down Anna looks down the table to see, yet again, Scott with ten bowls of stew and a mountain of bread. Anna looks around at all the people before her and just smiles; this is one of the happiest days of her life. She is surrounded by her friends and family, no more danger, no more evil creatures. Everyone is happy that Nightmare is finally gone and it seems like a veil was lifted from the village. After everyone ate it is time for the dancing to begin. The band takes hold of the instruments once more and begins to play. Groups of people dance with one another, forming circles and just danced about. Jack and Scott sit off to the side and just watch. Scott could barely move from how much he ate. He felt like a water balloon ready to pop at any moment so he just lies there on the log. Jack just laughs and feels someone pull him from the log. He pulls his hand to see Suki standing before him. She just laughs.

"Come, dance."

Jack just shakes his head.

"Come."

"I can't….um..too full from eating."

Suki just grabs him by the arm and pulls him into the crowd while Scott waves with a sarcastic smile on his face. Suki swings about him and swings him around in circles. They bump into other dancers and trip over other's toes. Suki just laughs as Jack dodges the others coming at him. Then the music slows down to a mellow tempo and many left the dancing area. Jack tries to sneak out, but Suki pulls him back in.

"Come Jack. Dance with me."

Jack looks around to see couples slowly dancing to the beautiful music. He gulps and takes Suki's hand and one around her waist. Suki leans her head on to his chest and sighs. Jack looks over to see Scott making kissy faces at him and laughing. Jack just glares back. He looks around to see Anna dancing with Vladmir. He feels a cold spot fill his heart. He watches quietly as Anna and Vladmir dance away from them. Jack looks down at Suki.

"Suki."

She looks up at him with curious eyes.

"May I go take a walk? I just need to get something off my mind."

Suki nods quietly and walks to the log that Scott is still lying on and Jack heads away from the crowd but is stopped when he hears the crowd gasp. He turns around to see Vladmir and Anna rising into the air dancing. He turns away and continues to somewhere quiet. Anna looks down and grips Vladmir tighter.

"Vladmir?"

"Yes?"

"You do know we are flying right now?"

Vladmir looks down to see that he is dancing above the villagers heads. He just smiles.

"Well, I guess that's my gift from the goddess."

They start to lower to the ground and the villagers part ways as they come closer to the ground, when they land Anna looks around to see that she is on the ground and looks up to Vladmir. Vladmir leans over and kisses Anna once more and the crowd cheers.

Jack has walked towards the training grounds. The thoughts in his head whirl about. He shoves his hands into his coat pockets and shakes his head trying to rid his mind of these thoughts. He comes to a log and sits down, the lies down on the ground. He stares up to the stars and watches them twinkle in the night sky. He listens to the soft sounds of nature around him. He feels the gentle wind blow past and the blades of grass brush against him. He closes his eyes and falls into a deep meditated state which unfortunately gets interrupted by someone laughing. He opens his eyes and sits up and listens for the laugh. Then he hears giggles coming from the edge of the forest. Jack stands up and heads to the forest edge. He listens and hears something rustle in the nearby bushes.

"Scott, I know it's you!"

Then a voice comes from the forest.

"Man, you ruined the surprise. I betcha you can't catch me. Hahaha."

Jack hears running footsteps go farther and farther into the forest. He takes off into the forest to chase down Scott. Jack dodges trees, branches, and holes in the ground. Scott laughs and Jack gets frustrated.

" Scott, this enough! Get back here before I pound you to a pulp."

Scott just laughs and continues into the forest. Scott's laughter gets louder and louder as Jack inches near Scott's location. Jack looks around to spot Scott but can't. He can hear him but can't see him. Jack emerges from the forest with Scott's laugh echoing around him. He looks about him to only hear himself panting.

"Scott, this isn't funny anymore. Come out before I pummel you!"

Scott didn't respond. Jack notices that he is in an open field. As he walks on Jack trips over something. He looks back to see a piece of the earth sticking out of the ground. Jack looks closer to see that this piece stretches from one side of the clearing to the other. A chill runs up his spine and his heart begins to race. Jack pulls out his dagger.

"Okay Scott you got me, now come out."

Jack turns quickly when he hears something rustle the grass behind. He turns to see a small shape in the darkness. He steps forward cautiously. Then the small figure throws something and glass shatters in front of him. A small smoke cloud rises and starts to emanate a green glow. Jack looks down as the small figure plops in his direction. When the figure comes into the light Jack takes a defensive stance.

"Hat."

Hat just smiles.

"What did you do with Scott? Where is he?"

"Where's Scott? Where is he?"

Jack backs away as Hat spoke those very words with Scott's voice. Dark whispers wrap around him. Jack turns and runs to the edge of the clearing and just as he reaches the forest's edge a force grips him by the leg and pulls him away. Jack digs at the earth with his hands and the dagger. Deep gouges scrape the earth as he is pulled closer and closer to Hat. Jack looks down at his foot to see a dark black hand pulling him in. He reaches down and strikes at the hand's arm to only go right through it. Then his foot drops and he gets up as quickly as he can. Jack tries to run again and is stopped by a black wall. He grips his dagger and turns to charge Hat. Just before he reaches Hat multitudes of black hands take hold of him. One of the hands takes hold of his dagger and throws it over the black wall. The hands hold him up so his feet are just above the ground. Jack glares at Hat and Hat just smiles.

"What do you want?"

"A host."

"What?"

"A HOST!"

Hat's voice became darker. Then evil laughter echoes around them. Jack watches as a black gooey mass pulls away from Hat. The laughter continues and gets louder. The dark mist clouds Hat out of Jack's vision so now all he sees is black. Jack looks around frantically and then the hands grip tighter around him. A hand comes up to the back of his head and forces him to look straight into the darkness before him. Jack tries to fight it with futile effort. Then right before him a pair of red eyes illuminates the dark mist. Then it lunges towards him with a shrieking ghastly scream. The black goo pushes into his skin and begins to flow into his veins. The hands release him as the black goo continues to force and crawl into his skin. The black mist that surrounds him swirls around him into a black snake and forces its way down his throat. Jack cannot do anything but feel the burning pain as the black ooze enters his veins. Then Jack just drops to the ground gasping for air. An agonizing pain races throughout his body. He looks down at his arm to see his skin peel away to reveal dark gray metal underneath. Three horns forced their way out from his forehead. He could feel three points start to protrude from the back of his head. Two small ones grow from behind on either side of his lower jaw and one big one from the crown of his head. His shoulders pop revealing crimson red armor. Sharp points shoot out from his elbows. Jack screams out into the night as his skin continues to peel away from him. Jack leans over from the pain as a voice echoes in his mind.

"He took her."

"He took her away from you."

"What?"

"She would have been yours if the *goddess* didn't bring him back."

"No...."

"She would have been by your side."

"No......."

"She should be yours."

"......"

"Help me and I will make sure of that."

"....."

A figure of metal now stands where Jack has once stood. Three horns protrude from its head and one large one from the top of its head and drapes down the back. Two smaller ones stick out from either side of its head. Small diamond slits of white replace his eyes and has no nose or mouth. A tattered and torn crimson red scarf flows about him in the gentle breeze. Crimson red spikes wrap around his knees and elbows with a single point jarring out. Upon his hands he wears dark brown gloves with silver bars across the knuckles and a brown belt around his hips. His shoulders now have deep crimson shoulder guards with four black pegs jutting out and the very edge of the guard is outlined in black. He stands and looks down at himself. He turns and walks towards where the dagger was thrown. He picks it up and it too begins to change. The handle stretches out to a long dark gray pole with a crimson red grip bar in the center with black crosshatch design. Towards either end of the pole two large scythe-like white blades grow facing opposite directions. On each blade, towards the top next to the pole, a small royal purple gem gleams in the moonlight. He takes the scythe at the center and pulls it apart to make two small weapons. He tries out the small weapons with strikes and attacks in the air. Then he places the pieces back together and hooks the scythe onto his back.

Upon the tallest hill in all of Azmala stands of figure of metal in the night. He looks upon the small village in the distance and listens to the cheering and sounds echoing into the forest. A black mist pulls away from him and looks out to the village.

"Azmala will fall to me. Darkness shall rule this land. My shadows will tarnish this land and no soul shall escape. Come, Toran, their end draws near."

The mist dissipates and Toran disappears into the shadows of the night.

END OF BOOK ONE